GRASSLANDS

GRASSLANDS

Stories by

JONATHAN GILLMAN

RUTGERS UNIVERSITY PRESS
New Brunswick, New Jersey

To those whose comments and feedback helped make this better, in particular Randeane, Susie and her old man, and, most especially, Elena, for her faith, encouragement, and time, my appreciation and my thanks.

Grateful acknowledgment is made to the following publications in which some of these stories first appeared: Azorian Express *("Cows Dying");* Pikestaff Forum *("The Cattle Buyer");* Albany Review *("The Wide Mizzou");* Potato Eyes *("A Bracelet of Bright Hair");* the Rockford Review *("Shakespeare by Phone");* The MacGuffin *("Bones" and "Midsummer's Night" as "Night"); and* Sidewalks *("The Old Days").*

Copyright © 1993 by Jonathan Gillman
All rights reserved
Manufactured in the United States of America

Library of Congress Cataloguing-in-Publication Data

Gillman, Jonathan.
    Grasslands / Jonathan Gillman.
        p.   cm. — (Rutgers Press fiction)
    ISBN 0–8135–1926–8 (cloth). — ISBN 0–8135–1927–6 (pbk.)
    I. Title. II. Series.
PS3557.I395G7 1993
813'.54—dc20   92–20988
                                                                               CIP

British Cataloging-in-Publication information available

For
Etta, in memoriam, who always believed
and Elizabeth, all ways

CONTENTS

Bones — 1980	1
The Gravedigger — 1978	4
The Wide Mizzou — 1976	11
The Old Days — 1975	21
Cows Dying — 1976	28
Stones on a Hill — 1979	34
Carny — 1987	41
Cliff Paintings — 1962	50
A Bracelet of Bright Hair — 1957	60
Killing Coons — 1972	67
Carny Man — 1960	73
Haying — 1977	90
Shakespeare by Phone — 1978	96
The House at South Webster — 1974	105
The Lake Monster — 1977	112
Artifacts — 1984	123
At the Fair — 1983	133

A Big One — *1985*	143
The Cattle Buyer — *1987*	149
Ed Blanchard — *1986*	159
Old Bones — *1988*	170
Midsummer's Night — *1989*	179
About the Author	187

GRASSLANDS

BONES

1980

Two nights before Christmas Mavis stopped at the Blanchard's. "I've come for bones," she said. "To make music with." Her breath hung white in the air. "Big ones would be better."

"I'll sh-sh-show you," Ed said. He was bundled into his jacket. Nothing showed but his face. He led her around the barn, down a trail. Their shoes crunched and squeaked on the snow.

They both had flashlights. The light reflected off the snow into the air ahead.

Above them stars jumped out of the sky.

Mavis stopped, staring up. In the distance the ice of a stock pond cracked. The sound seemed to echo off the darkness.

Ed pointed out the stars. "That's S-S-Sirius. The bright one."

"Is that the Big Dipper?" Mavis pointed at a group. Her breath disappeared into the darkness.

"No. Th-th-th-that's Orion. The Big Dipper's over th-th-there."

Her neck hurt from looking up.

Brilliant points of light surrounded them. The sky seemed immense.

They walked on. A deep hooting cut through the air. Ed stopped. Mavis waited for him.

He listened. The hooting boomed again. He looked out toward the sound, as if to address it. "It's okay," he said. "Sh-sh-she's a friend." He waited. The hooting sounded fainter.

He turned toward her. "C-c-come."

He walked further, stopped, turned, waded across a snowy field. Spears of grass pierced the snow.

At the edge he said, "Be c-c-c-careful. There's a fence." He pushed the wires down for her. "D-d-d-d-duck down."

It looked like he was leading her into a place of nothing but blackness.

She stepped forward, stopped, shone the flashlight around. She couldn't see stars or where they'd been.

She shone the light ahead on something white. It wasn't a shape she recognized. Ed stood on one of them. It was a rock.

He turned around, waiting for her.

She ducked under brambles, climbed on a rock beside him.

"Be c-c-c-careful getting down. There's old wire."

Around her Mavis saw pine trees, a grove, blackness. She stepped down onto a sheep's head, made a surprised noise.

Ed was ahead of her. "S-s-s-something's been here. Chewing on the c-c-c-carcasses. In the summer in three days there is n-n-n-nothing but hide. They stay whole all winter, in the cold."

Mavis looked around. She saw a sheep, a calf, another calf half on it, lying as if resting.

They didn't move. She kept checking to make sure.

"The b-b-b-big ones are underneath."

"You don't have any buffalo bones?"

He shook his head. "J-j-j-just cow bones. They're almost as b-b-b-big."

"Do many die?"

He shrugged. "S-s-s-Some do."

"Why?"

"Different things. They g-g-g-get sick. I don't know." He moved to the back, bent. "This was H-H-H-Hilda. She was my f-f-f-favorite." He turned his head away, reached down, squatting, touched a skull with his hand. He stood, broke off a sprig of green pine needles, laid it on her empty eye sockets.

He pointed at another. "Th-th-th-this calf died a month ago. Come on, girl."

He called her by a name Mavis didn't catch.

"We f-f-f-forgot to take her c-c-c-collar off." He grabbed her by it, slid her aside. "Th-th-there're the old ones."

Mavis shone the light down. A circle of bones lay scattered about. Ed nudged them with his foot. Some were frozen into the ground. He bent down, picked up two long ones, clacked them together.

"D-d-d-do they make the n-n-noise you want?"

Mavis nodded. "That's great."

"Here." He handed her two others. She beat them together. Clank clank.

He hit his two together. They made a different tone. Clink clink.

Clank.

Clink clink.

Clank clank.

In the dark, in the grove, they started a rhythm going.

Clink—clank clank—clink clink clink—clank—clink clink—clank clank—clink.

Mavis smiled as she clanked. She was fighting off the night.

THE GRAVEDIGGER
1978

My father died, widowed and remote. Nothing about it felt good.

After he'd retired, they sold everything, left Watervliet, took off with what remained of life in Michigan stuffed in a trailer behind them, drove south until they reached Florida. They hadn't been there long when mother died and there he was, alone in a strange place.

He hitched the trailer to his pickup, set off driving. He stayed a few days one place, moved on. I never knew if he was looking for a home or just passing through.

He visited us, stayed two weeks. It was great having him. He and Nate'd always got along, and he and Alice hit it off fine. The three of them spent days together fishing at the reservoir, having a high old time. But fourteen days passed and he had to be on the road again.

He started getting sick. We got cards from towns he was recovering in. "Ms M Johnson," he addressed them, "Over The Cafe, In the Heart of Grasslands, South Dakota."

"Dear Mavis," they always started in his shaky hand. Then something about the weather and how he was "under it," finishing up with "Staying a few days til it's past." And on the front, overdone pictures of the Wisconsin Dells, Kentucky Lake, Lake Pontchartraine, the Alamo, "oil wells in sight of the capitol, Oklahoma City." And small places I'd never heard of, had to get the map book out to find—Eunice, Oklahoma; Arvada, Colorado; Alamogordo, New Mexico. I wondered if I had a big wall map, with pins stuck in for every place he wrote from, if it'd make any kind of pattern.

He died in a small town in northern New Mexico. His truck'd broken down while he was camped with his trailer in the town park. I guess he decided to wait there until he got the part. I pictured it parked by a dry stream, next to a picnic table, under a lone tree.

Someone found my name in his papers. I wanted to go out and reclaim him, couldn't afford it. I had them send the ashes back in a box, dispose of the truck and trailer at public sale. I couldn't see anything in either of them that had any value for me.

I took his passing hard. So soon after Nate's. I thought of the waste, the things never done, how I'd felt about him that I'd never said. The last time he visited, I knew he was sick, I might not see him again. I kept touching him, wanting to hug him, to tell him I loved him. He just drew back, closed in on himself, like he couldn't hear it.

The night his ashes came, I set the sealed box on the kitchen table, sat up late, drinking wine, staring at it, trying to understand how a container less than a foot on a side could hold all that remained of my father and still have excluded the most important part.

I couldn't accept that he wasn't still in the box, squeezed down to fit inside. If I undid the lid, I imagined him popping out, as alive as ever.

After midnight, when the bottle was empty, I took the box and a pointed shovel out into the back, started digging next to the blueberry bushes. Three shovelfuls hardly scratched the surface. I tried another place; same results.

I leaned on the shovel, looking down at the box, its black sheen milky white in the moonlight. I bent down. From the beginning of a hole I took a handful of dirt, tossed it on the box. My fingers felt numb. The moon, clear on a sparkling night, looked fuzzy. I picked the box up, trying not to shake the loose dirt off, carried it back into the house, put it under a moth-ball-smelling sweater at the bottom of a closet.

I found it a month later when I was looking for a pair of shoes. I carried it out, laid it on the floor of the pickup, stuck the shovel behind the seat, left them there wherever I went—in case I ever found the right time and place.

I'd never buried anything except a cat that died when I was seven. I remembered the frustrations of digging, running into tree roots, moving to a softer spot, starting again. But I remembered too the feeling of completeness when I laid the stiff shape into the small hole and covered it with dirt.

Other memories of the cat came back. How, after I'd dug the hole, I held her against me, still warm, and scratched her ears, the way she liked. I kept holding her, scratching and scratching, not wanting her to get cold, not wanting to put her down. Even then I knew she was dead, to let me keep scratching. When I'd held her long enough, I put the old plaid blanket that she'd slept on in the hole, laid her down on it, dropped a green sprig on top of her, folded the blanket over her, started pushing dirt in.

And there'd been Nate. The empty hole filled in beneath a new stone by the church at the end of the street after they'd fished him out of the reservoir, water-logged and bloated.

A month later Mort and I had taken his ashes out on the boat. I'd sat in back, watching the water churn away from the propellor, wondering how the vibrations felt to creatures living below. I imagined the chug-chug-chug surrounding them, driving them deeper and deeper to escape it.

When we reached the place where they'd found him, Mort

stopped the motor, stood beside me. The boat bobbed up and down in the silence. I didn't know where we were. All I saw in any direction was water. I had no idea how deep it was, how far from the main channel we were, what was underneath—fields, valleys, trees, graveyards? Whatever it was seemed hidden forever.

Mort helped me pry the lid off. Nothing popped out. All the box contained was a few inches of ashes, settled at the bottom. We each took a handful, sowed them on the water. I don't know what I expected, for the ashes to congregate together or sink to the kingdom where Nate was trying to go. I was surprised to see them sitting like dust on the surface, scattering with the breeze all around, looking a little like the Milky Way against a dark sky.

When one of the few old people left died, I waited at the cemetery until Marvin Pembroke, Mort's father, showed up with his shovel.

I hid in the shadows, watching, while he dug. It could have been any hole, by the way he acted.

After a while I stepped forward, started asking questions.

"What do you think about while you're digging?"

"Nothing." Down the shovel went. Twist, he turned it, lifted it, brought it up. "How hard the soil is. How well the digging is going."

He emptied the shovel, returned it to the soil, stepped on it again. As the shovel dug deeper into the ground, I half expected him to toss out an old skull.

"Do you ever dig up the bones of other people?"

"Sometimes, if the old grave's not marked. Not too often though. There's lots of room here."

"Doesn't that bother you?"

"It's not something I like." He unloaded another shovelful. "But after they've been in here a while bones are bones. More likely to find old Indian doo-dads."

"Like what?"

"Arrowheads. Tomahawks, sometimes. Guess this was a meeting ground of theirs before the white folks showed up. That corner back there's like it was the dump, arrowheads all over the place. I try not to dig there if I can help it."

I looked around the small plot. Pembroke and Johnson were half the names.

"How do you feel about burying people you know?"

He leaned on the shovel. "No different, I guess, from anyone else that knew them." He went back to digging, always the same—step, push, lift, toss.

"What if the person was close to you. Or a relative. Have you ever done that?"

He nodded. "A lot of them won't, but I have. Old Olaf Nilsson, that was gravedigger before me. The first one I ever did." He pointed toward a stone in the corner near the road. "His wife died, not much before him. He couldn't bring himself to do it. Tried three times, and finally said, 'Marvin, could you? Soil's too damn hard today.'

"I didn't do too good a job. The sides were crooked, dirt kept falling back in, but I don't think he noticed." He paused. "If it was Gladys . . . that'd be hard. But I think I could, like I was doing the last thing in the world I could for her." He leaned into the shovel, tossed more dirt out. "But if it was Mort, or any of his kids . . ." He stepped on the shovel. "I don't know. I hope I don't ever have to."

More dirt flew out. "There are cousins I've buried. Good close friends. Even people I grew up with." Down the shovel went into the earth. "Hell, seems like most of the people I've known are in here by now."

"Isn't that hard?"

"It's sad work, sure."

"Don't you keep thinking about them?"

"No more than you would if they were anyone close. It's just you have more opportunity while you're digging."

I thought of the process, every shovelful a memory of the person gone.

"But the rest of them, it's only a box and a pile of dirt to shovel back in. Good ones, bad ones, you know their time is going to come. Once they get to you, there's not much you can do for them." He stopped again. "The worst ones are the children."

"Why's that?"

"For the promise in them, that never gets fulfilled. The box is only two, three feet long, but you know that hole is harder to dig than a full-sized one." He threw out two shovelfuls, stopped. "A couple of years ago, don't know if you remember, the little Oliver girl was hit by the car?"

I nodded.

"She'd been on my school bus the year before. I saw her standing there waiting to get on the whole time I was digging."

I pictured kindergarten girls in bright dresses standing by the side of the road. I didn't think I could've done it.

"Glad I don't depend on it for my livelihood. I'd'a gone broke ages ago. Only doing but three, four a year as it is. Guess you can tell a place is getting smaller when there's nobody left to die." He got a twinkle in his eye. "But there's one man in this town whose grave I will not dig."

"Who's that, Marvin?" I asked, wondering if I was going to find out about some old feud.

"My own." He smiled. "I might have to, though, if they can't find anyone to replace me."

"How would you do that?"

"Guess I'd have to plan ahead, wouldn't I?"

"Wouldn't that make you feel funny?"

"Depends on when it is. If it's soon, I guess I'd regret it. But if it was a while from now, I might welcome it by then. The worst thing'd be being so weak and frail I couldn't do a decent job of it. Can you feature what a mess that'd be, a gravedigger botching the last grave he digs."

After that, whenever I ran into him, or he stopped in at the cafe for coffee, he smiled. "I still haven't got my own dug yet. But every now and then I think about it."

I was out by nine o'clock the morning after Gladys died. I found their family cluster, started where I thought was best.

Marvin showed up at eleven. When he saw what I'd done he took my hand, squeezed it. He looked as if he wanted to smile but couldn't. "Thank you," he said. He kept saying it. "Thank you. Thank you."

The work was slow. The surface was hardest. The deeper I got the easier it seemed. Bend, push, lift, toss, slow and steady. There was lots of time for thinking—about the work, how it was going, how hard the soil was, how dry it was, when it'd rained last, how long it'd take, did I really have to go down six feet, why so far, how I'd ache the next day. About Marvin, and Gladys. How Mort'd take it. How lost Marvin looked, sitting off to the side, staring into space. Twice I held the shovel out, offering; he just shook his head.

I didn't find any arrowheads. Just baked dry dirt. I guessed I'd have to go back in the corner for that, save it for another day.

All the while the hole kept getting deeper—down to my ankles, down to my knees, down to my thighs. It looked like I was going to make it. All it took was time.

I wiped my forehead, wishing I'd brought water.

When I was finished, maybe I'd take a little rest, then start in on my father's, put it beside Nate's. But I didn't think the hole'd have to be so big, if all I was burying was a box.

THE WIDE MIZZOU
1976

"The Missouri, when combined with the Mississippi, forms the longest river in the world. Water that starts flowing in the mountains of Yellowstone National Park has, by the time it reaches the Gulf of Mexico south of New Orleans,"—Mort gestured, as if to indicate a place a long way off—"traveled as far as it is possible for fresh water to go in one continuous direction."

He stopped.

Mavis, lying between crumpled paper plates and dirty plastic forks, her hair against the almost empty bowl of potato salad, waited for him to go on, the outline of the river on a map vivid in her mind. Beside her on the blanket sat her husband, Nate, chewing a barbecued rib. Turning her head, she saw Mort, standing, sway as he took a swig from the bottle of wine in his hand.

"The entire Mississippi River system," he went on, from time to time slurring certain words, overemphasizing others, "comprised of the Father of Waters itself, all its major tributaries, many of them significant rivers in their own right, of which our own Missouri is one, and their increasingly smaller contributors, down to the little streams and intermittent brooks that are everywhere, stands like a gigantic tree spreading throughout the middle of the United States, with limbs, branches, twigs reaching from the Appalachians to the Rockies, and draining the entire area with a volume of water that is the fifth largest in the world."

Mort stopped, squinted down the hill where, Mavis knew, the rest of their party—her daughter Alice, his wife Carol, and Jerry and Jane, their two children—were little more than specks by the water.

Mort took another swig, held the bottle out toward Nate and Mavis.

"No, thanks," Mavis said.

Nate shook his head. "Ribs?" he offered in return.

"No more for me, thanks. I'm sticking to the grape." Mort raised the bottle, what remained of its contents purple in the sun.

"Just as the Mississippi," he continued, "is central to the United States, so the Missouri bisects South Dakota, running from north to south through the middle of the state, and dividing it into two quite distinct parts that mark, to the east, the end of the flat prairie grassland"—he pointed across the water at the unseen expanse of land to the right—"and the rougher, hillier plains of the west."

"It is on this land"—Mort spread his arms, encompassing all the land in sight—"that the buffalo were native, forming, with the short 'buffalo' grass, a perfect ecological fit. With all we've done since, in terms of cattle breeding and fancy genetics, the land still doesn't produce as much as meat on the hoof as it did back then when everything was just wild and wooly."

Mort examined the bottle. "I'm sure there's a lesson in that somewhere. If you feel like it . . ."

Nate stood up, stretched, looked down toward Alice on the bank, Jane and Jerry in the water, yawned, stretched again, sat back down closer to Mavis. She rubbed his hand, put her head on his leg while she listened.

"For years the river acted as a barrier, separating east and west. It wasn't until 1924 that a bridge was built across it, an event of such significance that the town that sprang up there was named 'Mobridge' for that very reason."

"I didn't know that," Mavis said from the blanket, looking up at Nate. "Did you?"

Nate nodded. "I grew up here too."

"Of the major tributaries to the Mississippi, the Missouri in its rate of flow was easily the most inconsistent. In late summer and fall it slowed to a trickle. In spring and early summer it swelled and flooded and rampaged, carrying thousands of tons of soil toward the ocean every year. That's why it was also known as 'Big Muddy.'"

He took another swig.

"To control this, the government built a series of dams all along the upper Missouri. In 1963, one of these, the Oahe Dam, 246 feet high . . ."

"That high?" Mavis interrupted, lifting her head. "It must have covered a lot of interesting country."

"It did," Nate whispered down to her. "A lot of people"—he nodded up at Mort—"said it shouldn't be built."

"246 feet high," Mort went on, "and 9300 feet across, was constructed just north of Pierre, forming the Oahe Reservoir"—he pointed at the water—"a lake that stretches north four hundred miles almost to Bismarck, North Dakota, and at its widest is fifty miles, though the main body is only five to ten miles wide. It is here, where the Cheyenne River enters into the reservoir, that we have taken advantage of its superb recreational opportunities to celebrate our country's two-hundredth birthday, instead of sweltering in Aunt Tillie's backyard with the rest of our relatives."

He took another swig.

"Therefore, my friends, on this historic occasion, I offer a toast." He lifted the bottle. "To the Missouri."

Nate raised his plastic cup. "The Missouri."

Mavis held up her empty hand. "The Missouri."

Mort took another long swig and sat down.

Mavis clapped. "Bravo. Excellent. That's the best Fourth of July speech I've ever heard."

Nate grumbled. "It's just South Dakota history, grades five, six, seven, eight, nine, ten, eleven . . ."

Mort, watching down the hill, waved when Carol turned toward him, seemed to say something.

She spoke again, he waved again. "In a bit," he shouted. "I don't feel like moving."

They sat quiet, picking at bones and potato salad.

Nate poured himself an inch of wine. "Almost out of wine."

"There's another bottle." Mort indicated the picnic basket. "Plus three more in the car. I don't think we'll run out."

Silence, like a bubble, surrounded them, then grew, until it encompassed the hillside, the water, the sky, the universe. They sat in the clear blue, warmed by the sun, made comfortable by the breeze. They saw without watching the blowing grasses, waving wild flowers, rippling, unmoving water.

A hawk circled their hill, his shrill whistle causing them to look up. Above, too high to hear, was the white trail of a jet traveling from somewhere far to the east to somewhere far to the west.

At the other side of the inlet a group of white pelicans flew slowly down, landed with a visible but silent splash, waded in shallow water near the bank.

A large snake, black against the water, swam toward the opposite shore. They noticed him when he was in the middle, charted his progress the rest of the way, zigging and zagging as he moved.

From time to time they heard Jerry's shouts and huzzahs as he played in the water.

"Did you know there are giant sturgeon in there?"

"In where?" Mavis sat up.

"There." Mort pointed toward where the snake had been.

Nate acted impatient. "Go on with your stories."

"There are. I was in Pierre last week when a man came in with one that weighed 326 pounds. He caught it two miles from here."

Nate scoffed. "Sure."

"I saw it. A huge, ugly thing. 'How old is it?' I asked. 'How long does it take to get this size?' No one knew."

"Is Jerry safe out there?" Mavis worried. "Don't go too far out!" she shouted. No one heard.

"Did you even know 300-pound sturgeon were in there?"

"No. And I'm not sure I believe you."

"I saw it. Its picture was in the paper. I still have the article. Remind me the next time you're down at the bank."

"All right, I believe you. There are 300-pound sturgeon all over the place out there. Now, Mr. Mort, I have a question for you. How did they get there?"

"What do you mean?"

"How did a fish of that size get into this reservoir?"

"How does a fish of any size get anywhere?"

"I mean, was it born here, or was it born in the ocean and then swam here?"

"It was a fresh water fish."

"Meaning it didn't come from the ocean," Nate reasoned.

"Besides, it had to be here when the dam was built," Mavis joined in. "And if it's been here that long, then it must be reproducing here. So it could have been born here too."

"Ok. All right." Nate stopped, but held up his hand, as if to prevent interruption. "What about long ago, before there was a dam, even before there were people. At those times you were talking about, in late summer and fall, when the river slowed to a trickle. What did this gargantuan water monster do then? Did it stay here? And, if it did, how did it survive?"

"There were pools and places of deep water all along the river."

"So it could've survived. Fine. But I still want to know where it came from to begin with."

"Where does anything come from to begin with?"

"What I mean is, was there a central focus at the beginning of evolution? Did all sturgeon come from the same one place, or did they evolve independently in lots of different places? And if they did, if they were here all along, what about during the glaciers? Were they here then? Was there even a river here then? And, if there wasn't, where did they go?"

"I think," Mavis answered, "that evolution happened all over the place. That the sturgeon could have started in the river, or in whatever water was here before the river, and been here all along."

"You agree, Mort?"

Mort, in the middle of a swig, nodded. "Sounds good to me."

"All right," Nate went on. "Let's talk about us. We're like the sturgeon. We live in a pluralistic society—no center, no one commonly held set of beliefs. Will you agree?"

"I'll drink to that," Mort responded, raising the bottle.

"Sounds good to me," Mavis answered with a smile.

"Ok. And here we are, we're celebrating our country's two-hundredth birthday by having a picnic, we're looking down at the dammed waters of the Missouri, and we're having a discussion about sturgeon, and the river, and us. Right?"

"Right," Mort answered. "What's your point?"

"My question is: is our conversation unique? Is this the only time anyone has ever had it, expressing the same thoughts and ideas . . ."

"Yes." Mort clunked the bottle of wine down on the blanket. "Absolutely."

"Why? You've got sturgeon doing the same thing all over the place. Why can't people?"

"Because people aren't sturgeon. Human beings are unique. Each and every one is unlike any other that ever existed or ever will exist. The products of their minds are unique; and so are their conversations. No one else has ever had this conversation, and no one ever will."

"I don't agree. I think it's quite likely that they have. That's what the lack of a central focus means."

Mavis broke the thoughtful silence that followed. "I don't know how likely it is," she said slowly, "but I think it's possible."

"So it could've happened. That's what matters." Nate stood up, cupped his hands, turned all directions of the compass. "Yoo hoo, out there, if you're having a conversation like this one, or if you ever did, or if you ever do, let us know, will you?"

He stood listening. The only answer any of them heard was the wind, blowing in small bursts.

He sat back down.

An uneasy silence ensued, each of the three pursuing his own thoughts until in the silence the uneasiness vanished, and they were left with the sun, the wind, the water, and the ground around them strewn with the remains of their picnic.

Nate yawned, stretched, but in no other way changed position. "Time for a swim." He stretched again.

Mavis lay on the blanket, her arm shielding her eyes. "I could stay here all afternoon." A warm breeze caressed her face.

Mort stared off into the distance. "What do you know," he started, turning toward Mavis, "about the Mandan?"

"The what?"

"The Mandan Sioux. Indians. You can't talk about the Missouri in South Dakota without talking about the Mandan."

"I thought we were done with that."

"I am talking to your wife."

"Sure. Fine." Nate made a show of lying down. "Let me know when you're done."

"I don't know anything about them." Mavis had opened her eyes and was watching Mort. "I don't even know who they are."

"Were. They're long gone. Done in by the same things that did in all the Indians."

"Who were they?"

"Sioux. But unlike other Sioux, who followed the buffalo over the plains, they stayed in one place, in the bluffs and hills along the river, farming the flatlands beside it when the spring floods receded."

Mavis sat up and pointed at the water. "Here?"

Mort nodded. "In 1961, when work on the Oahe Dam started, archaeologists went along the river collecting as much data about the Mandan as they could before the historical record was lost beneath the water forever. The summers after my sophomore and junior years of college I worked with them on the excavations. We found hundreds of artifacts, thousands of them. We took what we could, but we didn't have the time, or the money, to remove everything. And of course some of the records were impossible to remove. The paintings, for instance, scratched into the soft stone of the cliffs. They crumbled if you touched them."

Mavis opened her eyes wide. "What happened to them?"

"They're still out there, in the main channel, two hundred feet under water. They never did decide whether the water was more likely to preserve them or hasten their decay. As far as I know no one's gone back to check."

He paused. "I have a few items at home, if you want to take a look at them."

"Why haven't I seen them before?"

"You have," Nate piped up, "they're all over the place—in the living room, dining room, den, even in his office at the bank. You can't turn around without tripping on something of 'historical importance.'"

"The stone hoe on my desk you picked up the other day."

"That's from the river banks?" Mavis remembered holding it like any other hoe, as if she would cultivate crops with it. "How old is it?"

"No one knows. It could be 1160 or it could be 1860. There's no way of telling."

"They used the same tools over and over?" She stopped, looking at the distant point where the sky and water met. A people had lived in sight of where she was. Now they were gone, their ancient habitat entombed in water. In holding the hoe, an article of everyday living, she'd been connected to them and their past.

From below, Carol's voice could be heard, calling. Mort waved. "Coming." He pulled himself up, took another long swig of wine, held the bottle out toward Nate. Nate shook his head. Mort pressed the bottle to his lips, drained it, tapped the cork back in, tossed it into the grass behind the blanket, and headed down the hill.

Nate stood up himself, stretched, muttered something about a swim, asked, "You gonna stay here?", picked up his towel from beside the blanket and waded down through the grass, slowly becoming smaller. When he reached the bank, off to the side from where Alice, Jane, and Jerry were playing, he stopped, pulled off his clothes, laid them together, folded, in a pile, with his towel on top, and walked, naked, into the water.

Mavis watched as less and less of him was visible until with a plunge he disappeared beneath the surface.

She saw all this as clearly as anything she had ever seen. Also firmly fixed before her was a vision of the scene Mort had described of the banks of the Missouri, preserved as it had been when the Mandan Sioux lived there, and seen in a dull brown light in which nothing was vivid, exactly as a representation of Indians and Indian life might look in an exhibit in a large, dark museum, which, she realized, signified that she was seeing it through the water of the reservoir.

As she watched, she saw enter this scene a whole village of Indians, as they had lived, walked, worked, a hundred years before, sealed alive under the water with all the mundane daily events that comprised their lives.

In one place, a craftsman worked on a painting in the cliff wall. In another, a young man on a pony rode along the shore, a hawk held high in his right hand, its beating wings just missing his head. In the center of the village, three elderly men sat smoking. Near them, a young woman was nursing a baby.

On the shore, two young boys were fishing. Whenever one caught a fish, he threw it onto the shore, where a girl cut off its head, removed its entrails, and, using a stone hoe like the one Mavis had seen on Mort's desk, chopped them into the ground.

The smaller boy pulled harder on his line, making no progress. The second boy laid down his line, started to help. Together they could not move it. The older boy turned back and called. Others of the village left their ponies, pipes, hoes, babies, paintings, walked toward the two boys until the whole tribe gathered round, pulling as one, straining on the line in unison, going slack together and tense, slack and tense, until with a mighty heave they pulled out of the water a huge, ugly sturgeon, and stood, cheering and dancing around it, while it lay huffing and flipping on the shore, small puddles collecting beneath it.

THE OLD DAYS
1975

"Grandpa."

"Alice?" He sat up with a start, shook his head, looked at her. "What's that?"

"Talk to me."

"Aren't I, Sweetheart?"

"You keep falling asleep."

"I'm sorry." His eyes closed again.

"Tell me."

He sat up, opened his eyes. "Tell you what?"

"Tell me about the dinosaurs."

"Again?"

"I like how you tell it."

"Well, all right, Princess. I'm ready to give it a go. What do you say?"

"Grandpa, were there dinosaurs when you were little?"

"There sure were, Honey. They roamed the land so thick the ground shook whenever they went by. And they were so loud, people thought it was earthquakes."

"Really?"

"You better believe it. And the appetites they had! A herd of 'em'd devour a whole forest in a single afternoon. You heard of the Sahara Desert? That's where it came from. Used to be a forest, till a couple of them got in there."

"Were they really that big?"

"You bet your bottom dollar. They were so big, if I stood in our second story window, I still couldn't look them in the eye. Not to mention tasty."

"You didn't eat them?"

"We sure did, Sweetie. Dad took his gun down, said 'I'm goin' out to get us a little dinner.' He wouldn't shoot but one, left it layin' where it landed. Then mom went out, cut off what she needed. Dinosaur steaks! mmm, were they good. Sometimes we called 'em 'dinoburgers.' Believe that's where the word 'dinner' came from, if I'm not mistaken.

"There was so much meat on 'em, one of 'em'd feed a whole town for a week. If anyone was hungry, they just walked out and sliced off a hunk. And that was only a little one. Some of the big ones—why, there was one I heard of, fed the entire town of Pittsburgh PA for a month on that one carcass alone.

"And the biggest one of all—when they died, they rolled over on their backs with their feet up in the air. This one, it was so big, after they finished eating everything out of it but the bones, you know what they did with the rest of it? Left it laying right where it was and called it Yankee Stadium."

"Grandpa!"

"Is there a Yankee Stadium or isn't there?"

"Yes."

"How do you know?"

" 'Cause I've been there."

"Taken by who?"

"You."

"So."

"Why didn't you tell me then?"

"It slipped my mind. But I remember now."

"Was it really as big as Yankee Stadium?"

"Sure was, Honey."
"Did you see it?"
"Not in person, I didn't. But I saw it on TV."
"Go on."
"What? What did I say?"
"You're pulling my leg, Grandpa."
"My hands are over here."
"You didn't have TV when you were little."
"We sure did."
"That's not what they said in school."
"You believe what you hear in school over what your own grandpa tells you? When I was a kid, everyone had 'em. Then, well, the programs weren't so hot, folks just stopped watching them. Before you knew it, they forgot about 'em altogether. Then some young upstart comes along, finds one in his parents' attic, claims he invented it himself. Hey, what're you doing there, Sugar Plum?"
"Can't I sit in your lap?"
"I don't know."
"You used to let me all the time."
"Sure, I did, Sweetie, but . . ."
"We sat out here in the shade by your trailer."
"That's right."
"And I climbed into your lap."
"Un hunh."
"And listened to you tell me things, and watched the leaves on the cottonwood blowing in the wind."
"You remember all that, Cracker Jack?"
"I sure do."
"Yeah, but you know what, then you were no bigger than a minute, and now . . ."
"Grandpa!"
"What? What's that?"
"Why did you stop?"
"It ain't nothing. Just that sometimes—come on, girl, climb

up in your old grandpa's lap if you want. Only be careful, right there on my stomach. If you push on it—easy, girl."

"Are you all right?"

"Sure am, Sweetie. Just sometimes don't feel quite as spry as I used to. You're growing up, getting to be a big girl. Well, I'm getting older too."

"Grandpa!"

"I'm not lying."

"You were old before I was born."

"That's right. But I'm older now." A fit of coughing shook him. "It's okay. I'll be done in a minute."

After he stopped they were quiet, her leg swinging back and forth.

"You know about Lake Superior, Honey Bunch?"

"I do, Grandpa. Miss James told us about it. It's the biggest lake in the whole world."

"You've got a mind on you, Sweetie Pie, sharp as a tack. Did she tell you where it came from?"

"No."

"That lake is a dinosaur soup Paul Bunyan cooked up for his mother. Went out one night, added water to the bones, and in the morning, there it was. You don't have to believe it if you don't want, but that's what I heard."

She nodded. "Grandpa?"

"Yessum?"

"What happened to the dinosaurs?"

"Got shot."

"All of them?"

"Every last one. People had contests to see who could bag the most. Practically before you knew it they did 'em in. 'Course that's why there are stadiums all over the place."

They were quiet again, her leg going back and forth.

He felt more coughing coming on. He kept it down.

She was getting heavy on his legs, but he didn't want her to move.

"You know, Thimbleful . . ."

"What, grandpa? Why did you stop?"

"What? What was I saying?"

" 'You know, Thimbleful.' "

"That's right. You know, Thimbleful, you should learn the stories yourself."

"I know them."

"You do?"

"Sure, I do."

"Why do you always ask me?"

"I like how you tell them."

"Thanks, Termite." He hugged her. "I like telling them." He started coughing again. "If there are any others—it's all right—you want me to tell you, you should go ahead and say so. Damn this coughing anyhow." He finished, spit a little at the end. It made him sore in the chest.

His feet were asleep.

He leaned forward, trying to shift her weight, his cheek next to hers. " 'Cause I won't be here forever."

"You'll come back next summer. Won't you? Maybe by then I'll be so big you can sit on my lap."

He wanted to laugh, but it hurt.

"I don't know, Sweetie. Driving's getting harder, pulling the trailer all that way."

"Mom and I could come see you."

"You could, that'd be nice." He coughed some more, held the last spasm in.

"Grandpa?"

"Mmm." He sounded almost asleep.

"You've been alive a long time, haven't you?"

"Sure have."

"How long?"

He thought. "When I was born, my uncle made a wheel and put a box on it, so my mother'd have something to push me around in. No one'd ever seen anything like that before."

"That long?"

"Un-hunh. I remember the first time my father gathered wood and brought it into the cave so I'd be warm when I was sleeping."

"Not that long."

"Oh, yes. And even longer. When I started walking, my grandfather'd climb way up in the high trees and get bunches of bananas for me, and swing back down to the ground with them."

"That's a long time."

"Yes, Honey, it is. A long time."

They sat quiet together.

"You need to remember everything I told you, so when you get bigger you can tell your children."

"Why can't you tell them?"

"What if I'm not here?"

"I'll remember."

"That's a good girl." He smiled. Everything was peaceful. Only his legs hurt. "You'll be all right." He hugged her.

"Not so hard, Grandpa. I'm still not as strong as you, even if I am getting bigger."

"You should get down now, Sweetie. Grandpa's tired. He needs to rest."

She climbed down.

"Can I stay here with you? I promise I'll be quiet."

He nodded, closed his eyes. "Fine with me."

She wasn't quiet long.

"Grandpa."

"Mmm?"

"Were there really dinosaurs when you were little?"

"Sure, there were. Didn't I tell you?"

He opened one eye, looked at her. She was slouched down in her lawn chair, thinking.

His eye shut again.

"Grandpa."

"What's that?"
"When I was little there were dinosaurs too."
He opened his eyes. "Go on."
"There were. I remember. They were so big, if one stood south of town, the whole town was shady. And if it didn't move for three days, but just stood there—you know all the lakes?"
He nodded.
"That's where its feet were."
"Are you sure?"
"Sure, I'm sure. Why you just bet . . ."
He smiled, shut his eyes.
"Grandpa. Grandpa!"
"Hunh?"
"What's it mean, 'bottom dollar'?"

COWS DYING
1976

Dad and I'd been working on that fool barn cleaner all afternoon, trying to get it pulling like it should; we had the chain off and motor every which way, and tried it one last time. Still it wasn't running right, so we left it. He went back to the house and I started bringing cows in for evening milking.

The first two'd already gone in the barn. I was in the yard still, keeping after stragglers. I thought I heard them bellow. It sounded strange, not like heat but short and sharp, so I started walking toward them. Before I was there, another went in; it bellowed once, a long high loud one, and was quiet. It was definitely strange. I was running now.

The next ones, they came right up to the barn, started going in, then they were bellowing too, that same way. They turned around, came back into the yard, carrying on all strange ways, acting like one sick cow. There was a bunch now, standing there hollering; seemed like just when they got to the barn that sickness got them. They were wobbling, and hollering, and looking like they couldn't hardly stand up, and acting fit to die. I looked in the barn. There was three cows in there, laying in the middle section on their sides, with their bellies up, and not any part of them moving, not even their tails. They weren't breathing either, that I could see, or making a sound. A bit of foam was at the edge of the mouth of the one that was closest, and her tongue was lolled out one corner of her mouth. I didn't know but they might not be dead.

Could be Hilda was one of them. She was always first in, and I didn't see her nowhere in the yard. I couldn't go in 'cause here came some others up to the barn, and it struck them too, til it seemed like the whole herd just about was out there carrying on. I went tearing down to the house, burst right in like gangbusters.

"D-d-d-dad."

"What's ailing you, Ed?" That was Dad answering. He took two or three puffs on that pipe of his, smoothed his beard a few times, said it real slow.

He didn't want me interrupting him, always said it aggravated him. I couldn't help it, I hadda get it said: "S-s-s-something's killing cows. They're d-d-dying left or right."

He just sat there puffing on that pipe, like he hadn't heard a word. I couldn't stand there waiting, I'd oughta been getting back, see if more was died.

"Ed," he said finally, letting smoke float outa his mouth while he said it, "haven't I talked to you about interrupting?"

"Th-th-there's three of them dead."

"You're doing it again."

"Can't you see he's upset?" That was Edna talking. She's my sister.

"So are you, Edna." Two or three more puffs on his pipe. "You know how it aggravates me."

I oughta been back out by then.

"What's wrong, Ed?" she asked.

"There's three of them dead on the floor of the barn, and most of the rest of the others, they're out in the yard, bellowing like to die, and looking it too."

"You don't know what it is?"

"Don't look like nothing I ever seen before."

"Not jimson poisoning?"

I shook my head. "Don't look it to me. They were all full and healthy when they came in the gate, 'cause I noted them, and the next thing, they bellowed and lay down and died, at least the one I seen did, 'cause I was out in the yard after stragglers and didn't see the two, but the one, it kind of bellowed and staggered, and then it was dead." And I staggered to show them, and bellowed too, and fell down to one knee.

Edna, she was up, slipping on her rubber boots, but Dad, he just sat there, puffing on that pipe.

"I oughta be gettin' back."

"You go on then, Ed," Edna answered, "and thanks, you did a real good job. We'll be right there."

I went running back. There was no more that died, but those in the yard were still carrying on like anything. In another minute, here came Dad and Edna. I don't know how she lighted a fire under him, but she sure did, 'cause he was chugging along good, and with her right behind, saying, "Doc Chandler's on his way, he'll get here as soon as he can," and both of them going, "Oh, no!" when they first saw them, and stopping, looking puzzled.

"Easy, Flossie, easy; it's all right, girl."

Both looking at ones that were bellowing worst. It seemed like maybe a dozen of them were acting sicker. The others, they were standing together off by the gate, not making any noise more than normal. I still ain't seen Hilda. Right about then Doc drove into the yard; you could hear him coming a mile down the road. He turned into the yard and screeched to a stop. He was over looking at the nearest sick one before the motor finished coughing.

"Is it something they ate?"

"What?"

"What else could it be? Are they getting worse?"

"Ask Ed; he found 'em."

They all looked at me, wanting an answer. That is one thing I don't like, makes me forget all what I was thinking. They still stood looking at me.

"N-n-n-no." I finally got that out. "And not better, neither. A-a-about the same."

"They gonna make it?" Dad looked worried, and you can know my father one long time before you see him look worried. Wasn't puffin' on his pipe, neither; must've gone out, and he stuck it in his pocket, and I know that wasn't frequent.

"Depends on what it was. I'll drench 'em, assuming it was something they ate. Can't do them any harm."

So we dosed them, all that was bellowing. It mighta helped a little, 'cause they wasn't making so much noise, and they sure didn't look so near to dying.

"Some died, you said?"

"Three."

"Where are they?"

Edna pointed to the barn.

"Bring one out and we'll take a look at it."

Dad got the tractor. All of us gave a hand hooking up the closest one. He hauled her out. That's when I got my first good look at her. It was Hilda. Born right there on the farm, daughter to old number seventeen that we hadda replace.

Seeing her, I remembered the times we wrestled and romped and she went jumping around, when she was still on bottle, not much bigger than me. Tears came into my eyes. I had to swallow hard to hold 'em back. Or I was in there, playing with her, after milking. If Dad was looking for me, I heard him and Mom talking, when she was still living.

"Have you seen Ed?"

"Did you look in with Hilda?"

"No."

"I would. 'Cause he sure does like that cow."

I remembered nights spent in the stall with her, when she was sick and we didn't know if she was gonna make it.

I used to think, "Ed and Hilda, they're friends." Even when

she was growed and off with the others, when I called she was there first, and I always saved bad apples and cores for her.

After we got her out where Doc wanted, I turned away, so no one could see I was just about crying. I went off to the other end of the yard, a lump the size of my fist in my throat. I was fighting to keep it down. I thought about sleeping in the stall with her, and the smells, the fresh milk, and the hay, and her warm calf smell, and even the manure. I thought maybe I'd sleep in there tonight, smelling those smells, and thinking it might be she wasn't gone just yet, but out in the pasture with the others. After a while I didn't feel so like crying. I walked back to where the others were.

Edna, she did a nice thing. She came beside me, and, little as she is, she put her arm up on my shoulder, and she said, "It's all right, Ed; I understand."

I couldn't think of anything to say, so I nodded, and was like to start crying again.

They had Hilda all laid out; Doc had her stomachs out, and her heart, liver, and kidneys, all her workings, looking at them. He couldn't find a thing wrong with any of them.

"Healthiest damn cow I've ever seen dead," he said.

That's just what I thought, bringing them in.

Dad dragged the other two out. It was the same with them. Doc, he said he was more perplexed now than when he first got there. Edna, she didn't know. And Dad, he wasn't saying nothing, except maybe thinking about three of his best milkers gone.

"It's a mystery," Edna said.

"Cows don't die of mysteries," Doc was saying, "they die of causes."

All of a sudden I knew, it was there in my head, and I said it, without thinking about it like I do most times, wondering if people are gonna laugh when I talk: "It's the barn cleaner."

Doc and Edna, they looked at me like they didn't know what I was talking about, 'cause they didn't. But Dad, he looked like he did. He shoulda too, all the time we spent working on it. We'd had the power on, seeing if it was fixed. We musta left it on when we went away, running into the water in the trench. When the cows came walking over the metal cover, "They were elect-, electro—"

"Electrocuted?"

That's what it was. That's why they were all right outside, and just inside they were bellowing.

I went to check the switch. Sure enough, it was still on, and I shut it off.

Doc Chandler, he said it satisfied him. He said the only reason we weren't killed ourselves was the cows were so big, they drained all the charge to them; that and the rubber boots we were wearing, 'cause otherwise every last one of us, when we helped him hook them up, we'd 'a been killed too.

Edna, she said it seemed that way to her too.

But Dad, he never said nothing, even though it was him turned that power on and was supposed to shut it off.

And to this day he still hasn't said not one word about it, or apologized, or anything. And I sort of think he should.

STONES ON A HILL
1979

Mavis drove north from town. She hadn't gone far when Nate appeared in front of her, just past the end of the hood, as if floating over the road. She sped up. She slowed down. There he remained. She took the next right, the left after that, the left after that, over roads she'd never seen before. He stayed right with her.

It'd been two years. She hadn't forgotten him. Every waking moment, it seemed, she wanted to find and join him. Why was he there? What did he want?

She had first seen him earlier that afternoon. It was Sunday, the cafe was shut. Something had impelled her into its darkened room. She stepped in and heard his voice. She looked toward the sound, saw him, full-sized, as if alive, standing in the corner by the front door.

"What?" she thought, not sure if she'd said it. "What is it?" She walked toward him, arms out in front of her, smacked both hands against the corner of the wall.

He hadn't left. She turned, saw him framed in the doorway she'd just come in. "What?" she said again, this time out loud. "What is it you want?" Her voice echoed in the empty cafe.

He was gone from the door when she reached it, stood in the kitchen in her apartment above the cafe, disappeared as she approached him, appeared again in the bedroom, seemed to fly out the window on the breeze, blow toward the vacant lot across the road. She looked out, saw only grasses blowing in the wind.

After that she'd grabbed the keys, hurried downstairs, climbed into the old green pickup, and headed north, averting her eyes as she drove past the cemetery, last night's flowers already faded at the base of his stone.

She was five minutes out of town when he caught up with her. There was no escaping him. She turned a fifth time; he was still in front of her.

The truck crested a hill, sped up as it began the decline, sputtered and slowed as it climbed. She put her foot on the brake, stopped at the top. Dust enveloped the cab, moved forward over the hood.

With both hands she held the steering wheel, stared down at the instrument panel. Beneath her the truck rumbled and vibrated. She shifted into neutral, pulled up the emergency brake, took her foot from the foot brake. The truck didn't move. She pushed the door open, climbed out, squinting at the brightness of the sandy road. She looked up, from one side to the other, back toward the front of the truck.

Nate wasn't there, only a few particles of dust scattering in the air.

She took a deep breath, looked around again, more slowly. She reached in the open door of the truck, put her hand on the key, switched it off.

Everything was still. She took a few steps away from the truck, its open door jutting into the middle of the road behind her, stopped, closed her eyes, leaned back her head, listened. The silence was immense.

She breathed in, smiled.

She opened her eyes. Still no Nate.

Mavis smiled again, started walking along the edge of the road. The wind wove a path through the alfalfa. A meadowlark sang, swaying on the top of a stem of tall grass. She was startled by the raucous call of a pheasant cock, hidden in a tangle of grasses. The wind died for a moment. From lower places she heard the trilling of red-winged blackbirds. Beyond the top of the hill, cresting and moving in every direction toward the horizon, she saw nothing but other hills, covered with grass, rolling into hills covered with grass. At the edge of sight they merged with the blue sky, dotted with puffs of white.

She began picking flowers—daisies, black-eyed Susans, wild sunflowers, a variety of others she didn't know the names of. She stopped before the salsify, its head a perfect collection of seeds, arrayed like a dandelion's but several times larger.

She took its stem between two fingers, with a twist lifted it toward her. At the motion, half a dozen seeds broke from the ball, floated away. Most of them traveled a few feet, landed on the tops of nearby grasses. One caught the draft of a gentle breeze, flew up over the road. She followed it until she could no longer see it, riding its umbrella of strands as fine as a spider's web.

She shook the remaining seeds off the head, blew away the last one, watched them sail away on a gust of wind.

She found another seed head. As gently as she'd ever laid Alice down, when Alice was small and colicky and the slightest jostle might wake her, Mavis separated the stem from its base. She held her breath as she lifted it toward her, added it to her bouquet. She placed it in the middle, its head standing above the tops of the other flowers.

When she'd collected as many as she could find, Mavis moved back toward the truck, looking for species she'd missed. Off to her right she glimpsed what looked like a bit of metal. Holding her bouquet up, she waded through the long-stemmed grass. It tickled her arms, caressed her waist.

She stopped, ten feet from the road, against a black, wrought iron fence, two feet high. It formed a square, hidden in the grass, twenty feet by twenty feet. To her left she found a small gate, open and unmovable. She walked in.

She had gone a few feet into the enclosure when her foot banged against a hard object. She looked down. Half covered by grass was an old cemetery marking stone. "Nate!" she said, surprised.

She looked around. She was nowhere she'd been before.

"No," she reminded herself. "His stone is in town."

The letters of his inscription drifted before her. "At the age of 57." The head of a salsify waved in front of her. "May he rest in peace."

Several umbrellas broke off, blew away. One came to rest on the top of another stone, settled so lightly, as if the slightest puff might lift it back into the air. A pocket of warm air floated by. The umbrella didn't move.

She took a deep breath, continued exploring the area she was in. She walked slowly, her eyes down. With one hand she held her bouquet up, with the other and a foot separated the grasses. She found a third stone, a fourth, a fifth. When she thought she'd seen them all, she uncovered a sixth. They stood at various angles, blanched by the sun and weather.

Two were normal size. Four were half height, the stones of children.

Whose markers were these? When had they lived? where? how had they died? She looked around. She saw nothing in any direction but sun, grass, sky.

Pushing the grasses farther apart, she saw writing cut into the stones. She knelt in front of them. With difficulty she made out what time, the wind, rain, snow and the constant rubbing of grasses had not obliterated.

A lamb was engraved at the top of each child's stone, beneath it "Rests in God," beneath that a name and dates. Hans. Helen.

Mary. The infant Christian. Aged six. Five. Three. And one. They died within a few months of each other—Christian and Helen in the same month, June. The year, 1897. Of what, she wondered. An epidemic? She tried to think what diseases were common then—measles, maybe, or influenza. These children may have been among the first white settlers there, but even their isolation offered no protection.

She thought of her own daughter Alice—at six, at five, at three, at one. At each age she imagined turning a corner to find sprawled limbs lying still. At each stone she knew the grief of the parents.

She moved to the stones of the parents. Harriet Ingevort, 27, dead also in 1897, after the last of the children.

By himself, to one side, Pietr Ingevort remained, dead twenty-five years later, aged 56. Mavis felt his loneliness, his anguish—to live so long in sight of these stones, in this place of beauty and desolation so intertwined it was impossible to think of one without the other.

She saw his life stretching out before him, day after day, year after year—always too much work, never completed, beating him, buffeting him, wearing him down. And then, if he wasn't defeated, hadn't given up, along came droughts and grasshoppers, hail and floods. Why did he bother going on? It was like trying to plow the wind. People were not meant to thrive there.

At that moment life made sense. No matter what, at one or fifty-seven, it ended here. It had no purpose, added to nothing. Not for her.

Not for Pietr.

Not for Nate. He was dead. No amount of wishing or pretending could change that. She needed to accept it. She had no choice.

She shut her eyes, thinking how to bid him farewell, trying to form the thought. She mouthed the words, opened her eyes, said them out loud. "Good-bye, Nate." She pulled the salsify from her bouquet, waved it back and forth until all the seeds were gone. "Good-bye!" she said, louder, as the last one drifted away.

She lifted what remained of her bouquet into the air over Pietr's stone, made the sign of a cross with it, laid it on the ground beneath the letters of his name.

She straightened up, looked around. Her mouth opened at the brilliance of the day. Her temples throbbed at the intensity of the colors—the blue of the sky, the white of the light, the green of the grasses.

She smiled at a scent of alfalfa, the trill of a red-winged blackbird.

She was still alive.

"Yoo-hoo," she shouted, "I'm alive!"

She listened. Nothing answered. The breeze, the hills, the sky swallowed the sound. Everything was still.

She wanted to take this moment home, keep it sealed in a jar on her kitchen table, where its glow would sustain her. She reached out toward the sunlight, the sound of the meadowlark, the salsify, closed her fingers tight around them.

She knew, without looking, she held only a handful of air.

Marvis waded back to the road, climbed into the truck, pulled the door shut behind her, started it, took one final look toward the plot, and drove off.

She crested the hill, started the long descent. At the bottom water lapped at the shoulder of the road. She stopped, sat in the truck a few feet from the inlet formed between the two hills. Sunlight glistened on its surface.

She couldn't understand the scope of the reservoir—how it rushed to fill the low places, adding miles at a time, its level still rising from runoff in mountains a thousand miles away—how it reached fifteen miles to the edge of this road, stretched straight across for forty, north for three hundred, over land it had covered inch by inch, year by year.

She thought of Nate—of his ashes, scattered over this water, now settled beneath it. She thought of other life that lay hidden beneath it. Of the Ingevort house, by a stream in what had been a hollow, with a few cottonwoods around. Of other houses, other lives. Of the stones in other plots. Of all who had lived and perished and been buried, and now where they lived and were buried was buried too.

She thought of the Mandan Indians, living for hundreds of years along the banks of the river. Of any others who might have come before them. Of every creature that had ever lived on the hills and in the hollows. To her mind, that life still remained, sealed intact by the water. It continued undisturbed, if only she could find the way to enter it.

She was disoriented as she drove up the next rise, came over the crest, started the decline. The water she saw in front of her seemed the natural entrance to the world she was seeking. As she sped down toward it she was startled awake by the contrast between the kingdom of water waiting for her and the brilliance of the day around her—the sun on her arm, the call of the pheasant in the grass to her side.

The second time he squawked, too close and loud to be anything but real, she jammed on the brakes. Her hands locked on the steering wheel. The truck slid sideways on the dirt and stones. Dust rose behind it. It came to a stop with the wheels a foot deep in water that, without warning, filled the hollow between the two hills, and that the wind, blowing by, made appear to be flowing.

On the hill ahead Mavis saw the road emerge from the reservoir a quarter of a mile away. It moved off as if there had been no change.

For a long time she sat, her hands tight on the steering wheel. She looked down at the murky brown water, lapping back and forth beneath the cab, looked ahead at the road sinking beneath the surface. She wondered why she had stopped.

CARNY

1987

The road came around the curve, straightened out. The fair spread out in front of her across the flat lands north of Pierre.

Mavis's stomach flipped over at the sight. She took her foot off the accelerator; the truck slowed. She pulled to the edge of the road, stopped, staring at the ferris wheel, a swirl of color turning above the horizon. She watched it stop, turn, stop, too far away to hear.

She hadn't been going to go. She had thought about it every day since March. She was going to stay away. But here she was, the sixth of September, most of the way there.

She started up, turned the truck back onto the road, staring ahead as she drove.

For two weeks she'd been thinking Alice would show up. She had imagined her tread on the wooden backstairs, the spring in her step, the way she seemed to bounce, even when she was tired.

The week of the fair she half expected to hear the door open, her voice call, "Hi, Mom, I'm home."

The fair opened Thursday. Sunday, Monday, Tuesday before,

Mavis thought of Alice all day, left the back light on when she went to bed, lay staring at the ceiling until fatigue overtook her.

"No," she decided when she woke in the morning to the empty apartment. "She couldn't have come yesterday. They haven't got here yet."

Wednesday Mavis sat in the chair by the phone all night, the light beside her on. Beneath it lay *The Complete Plays of Shakespeare*. She had taken such delight in it in the past. Now she never opened it. There was nothing in it, she felt, to help her through this.

Every hour she started from dreams showing variations of Alice returning, smiling, laughing, disappearing, coming back again. When she opened her eyes to sun streaming in the window, her hand was asleep, her neck sore and stiff. She was exhausted.

Thursday Alice didn't call. Or Friday. Or Saturday.

No one stopped by the cafe to say, "Been to the fair yet? Guess who I saw out to it yesterday? What a young woman she's become."

Sunday when she woke up Mavis knew she had to go see for herself.

She busied herself cleaning the spotless apartment, put off going as long as she could. Still she parked in the grassy field before noon. Getting out of the truck, she was startled to see the ferris wheel towering over her, turning to the rhythm of a recorded organ.

She tried to treat this like any other year at the fair. She walked around as she always had, looking at exhibits and displays; crafts, gadgets and technology; things hand made, things expensive and things cheap; the gleaming farm equipment, looming over everything; the livestock—chickens, rabbits, geese, sheep, pigs, cows; the ribbons and judging; the vegetables, familiar and obscure.

She tried not to remember that this was the first fair she'd come to alone. She tried not to think about the carny, kept glancing in its direction. She saw people coming from it holding large stuffed animals, caught glimpses between the buildings of the ferris wheel. Even when she turned away, she still heard the shrieks of children from the top and the constant drone of the hurdy-gurdy music.

She stood for ten minutes in front of a prize pig. A voice beside her said, "Big, hunh?" She had no idea what he was talking about. She was staring out the open window above the pen, watching the ferris wheel spin around and around, bright and colored against the blue sky.

Mavis felt sad walking toward the carny. "Alice isn't here," she kept telling herself. "Don't expect it." Her mouth felt dry, her stomach tight.

The carny had always made her feel uneasy. She wasn't sure why. It seemed too crass, too coarse and cold and hard. Everything had a price and it wasn't very high.

As she approached it she walked by booths of costume jewelry—hundreds of rings, belt buckles, bumper stickers, patriotic messages, only ninety-nine cents, a dollar ninety-nine, two ninety-nine tops, none of them worth even that.

She passed a man offering to guess your age, what kind of car you drove, the town you were from. "Only a dollar, win a beautiful prize if I'm wrong. What about you, my friend? How bout you, young lady?" The crowd around him wondered how he did it, urged each other to try.

The carny itself was divided into two alleys, with booths, displays, games—take-a-chance, hit the duck, knock over the bottle, make a hoop—leading down toward the Loop-de-Loop, the Bump Mobile, the Whirling Dervish, and in the middle, as if surveying both alleys, the ferris wheel.

Mavis started down one of the alleys, stopped. The noise and smells assailed her. She turned away.

She caught sight, outside the fence, of the village of campers and RVs the carny workers called home. From one of the campers she heard a woman's voice singing a country song, how someone had left her all alone, and she was just sittin' in a bar till he came home. She shut her eyes, trying to hear it above the noises of the carny. The voice sounded a little like Alice's. She stood listening. She couldn't tell if it was recorded or live. She was about to walk toward it when the singing stopped.

Mavis didn't want Alice to be there, didn't want to know it if she was, wanted to pretend she had a better life somewhere.

She turned around, looked back at the fair, placid and calm behind her, started toward it, stopped, turned back toward the carny.

She walked toward the first booth—"Three tries, knock five bottles down, only a quarter, win a beautiful stuffed animal"—as if the woman running it would be Alice.

She wasn't.

Mavis turned, looked across the alley at a shooting gallery. Alice wasn't there either.

Down the alley Mavis walked, half expecting Alice to be standing at the next booth, wearing a dark apron, taking people's money, making change. She wondered if Alice would acknowledge her, what she would look like, if her eyes would still sparkle, or if she'd seem as hard and tired as everyone else who worked there.

Booth after booth Mavis felt relief when the person tending it wasn't Alice.

At one, shoot three hoops, win the same old tacky stuff everyone tried to pretend had such value, Mavis stood a long time, watching the young woman running it. There was something about her, her curly blond hair, her bouncy manner, that reminded Mavis of her daughter.

The woman caught her eye. "You wanna try, lady? Only a quarter."

"Just watching," Mavis started to say. Her voice caught in her throat. She shook her head, felt tears on her cheek, turned away, walked on more slowly.

It was a beautiful day—clear, bright, pleasant. Mavis didn't care. She took no delight in anything.

In front of the next booth she stopped, staring into space, imagining Alice as a carny.

She thought of Alice at the fair the year before. How unfocused she had seemed, how restless.

"I think I'll go watch the girls at the horse show," Mavis had suggested.

"See you later."

"You don't want to do that with me?"

Alice made a face. "Yeah. Right."

"Last year you would have."

"That was last year."

"You're sure?"

"Come on, mom. Give it a break. I'll be down at the carny. If you're looking for me."

Mavis hadn't gone to the Horse Show. Thinking about the girls, riding in nervous, riding away deflated, their hopes and dreams gone with them, made her sad. And it was too near the Ox Pull. When she thought of Ed, not there again this year, her chest hurt.

Mavis had tried going only to safer places. That had become more difficult. Larger parts of the world she lived in haunted her, dredging up memories she couldn't deal with.

She had visited the embroidery exhibit, brightly colored quilts hanging from the walls. They only reminded her of the beautiful one Nate had said he'd buy her—"Next year, when we have the money"—the fall before he washed ashore.

All day Alice had hung around the carny. She was fascinated by the people, asked all sorts of questions about them, the life they led, where they spent the winter, what that must be like, going to a new town every week, and if you got bored with it, just a few days more, and on to some place else. She made it sound so romantic.

It seemed terrible to Mavis, going on and on the same, "Only a quarter, fifty cents, step right up, hit the target, win a prize, sorry, who's next, try again."

She didn't find Alice at any booth.

By the second alley she didn't want to look, knowing she'd be more depressed if she did find her.

Mavis was fascinated, and bothered, by the carny workers, their lives so different from hers. Where is the poetry in theirs? she wondered. The real magic, not just sleight-of-hand foolery? All they had was change. After a while, even that must seem the same, each small fair like the last one, the customers little more than quarters handed over for another chance at winning something they wouldn't pay a dime for elsewhere.

Mavis felt she didn't belong there. If Alice wasn't there, she had no connection to anyone, not to the workers or to the people trying their luck.

She walked by the last of the booths, no longer looking at them, stood in the open space between the two alleys. She watched people line up, wait, climb on the ferris wheel, be fastened in, move half a circle, stop, move a few feet, spin around, shrieking as they came over the top, holding on tight, stop, get off. Many of them got back in line.

She remembered going on the ferris wheel the fall before Nate died. Alice was seven. She was the one who had insisted on it. They had been fastened into the seat, with Alice snug between them. The wheel turned a few feet, stopped, another seat filled, while theirs rocked back and forth.

She hadn't liked any of it. As it lifted, her stomach dropped; as it dropped, her stomach lifted. There was one point in each half circle where her stomach, going up or down, caught up with where it was supposed to be. Going over the top she gripped the bar, felt she was about to be sick. And here people got back in line to do it over and over.

Watching one seat rise, stop, rise, stop, until it stopped at the top, she remembered being in that seat, the chair swinging back and forth, with the fair spread out below her, neat and clean and small. Looking out, to the west, she had seen the hills rolling toward Grasslands. To the north, she'd had to point, ask Nate, "What's that?"

It was the Oahe Dam, stretching across and up, so much bigger than she had thought. Behind it lay the reservoir, a huge volume of water. If she could see straight through it, she had decided, she would be somewhere in the lower middle, with a hundred and fifty feet of water above her. And if the dam broke, she remembered thinking, she and Nate and Alice and the ferris wheel and all the rest of the fair would be washed down the Missouri.

In front of her the ferris wheel turned around and around.

It hurt her to remember the next year, after Nate was gone. She'd ridden on the ferris wheel one last time with Alice, a lump in her throat the whole time.

Sitting on it she had taken out of her purse the bag containing the handful of Nate's ashes she hadn't scattered over the water. As the wheel turned over the top, she had shaken them out over the plain. A fine dust had rained on the people below.

Now she stood staring at the ticket taker. She was sure she'd seen him before.

He'd been there the year before, she realized. He was the one Alice kept talking to.

From that distance he was striking—dark hair, tanned, six feet tall, thin but not skinny, dark in his blue work shirt and pants. She felt a tingle on the inside of her thighs. Everything he did had a bored nonchalance that struck her as sexy. No wonder Alice had left.

She remembered wondering the year before, when Alice had gone back the Fair's last evening, if this was where she was coming. The next afternoon, when all the booths and games and the ferris wheel itself were folded up and the caravan of campers, trailers, RVs and pickups pulled out of town, headed for Aberdeen, Sioux Falls, or Valentine, Alice hadn't come home. Mavis wasn't surprised.

Maybe that was Alice she had heard in the camper, singing her own sad song, waiting until people left and he came home.

Mavis watched him more intently. When the seats were full, he pushed levers this way and that, started the wheel moving, stepped back, pulled a flask from his right rear pocket, took a long swig, another, spit, put it back in his pocket, stared off into space. As if an alarm had rung in his head, he pulled a lever, started the wheel slowing down, stopped it, let the riders out and the next ones on, a seat at a time, moved it a few feet, let out the next seatful. When the exchange was complete, he pulled the levers, the ferris wheel turned at top speed, the new riders shrieked, he spit, pulled out the flask, took a swig, shook it, called to someone, took another long swig, draining it.

He called again. Mavis held her breath.

A teenager emerged from behind the ferris wheel, thin, dark, tall, a younger version of him.

Without a word the man handed him the flask, the kid took it and left, the man pulled the levers, the shrieks subsided, the wheel slowed to a stop, a new group of riders climbed on.

After the wheel started again the kid came back, handed the man the flask, disappeared back behind the cables and machinery under the ferris wheel.

The man took a swig, spit, put the flask back in his pocket.

Mavis lost track of how long she watched. The ferris wheel loaded, spun around, unloaded, loaded, spun around, unloaded. The line at the beginning never seemed any shorter. Tall, short, fat, thin, young, old waited their turns, some carrying blue stuffed rabbits and white stuffed bears, eating cotton candy or candied apples.

Mavis felt she could have stood there all day, watching the wheel go around and around, knowing, in a way, all she wanted about Alice, in another not knowing anything.

She turned to go. Behind her the shrieks, the organ, the shouts continued. She saw in her mind the people open their mouths as they came over the top.

She turned back. When the next batch started, she walked toward the wheel until she stood before the ticket taker.

"It's full," he said, without looking at her. His twang surprised her. "Stay in line till next time." His breath smelled like whisky. There was a scar across his left cheek from his chin almost to his ear.

"Alice around?" she asked.

He turned his head toward her. "Who?" His eyes didn't focus on her.

"Alice Johnson?"

His face showed no recognition.

"Nobody I know of."

She nodded, muttered, "Thanks."

He pulled out the flask, took a swig.

She walked away, stopped at the beginning of the alley, looked back. She saw a woman, dark hair, short, bulging in her jeans at the hips, seem to come out from the machinery, hand him a sandwich and a beer, go back under the levers and cables. They didn't speak.

The man set the sandwich and beer down on the gear box, transferred riders, started another circle of giggles and shrieks.

Mavis turned, continued walking down the alley. As she left the carny she stopped, looked back one more time at the ferris wheel, going around and around, its colors painting swirls in the sky. It seemed slower, seen from a distance, and somehow not so important.

CLIFF PAINTINGS
1962

For two summers during college Mort worked on the expedition to preserve artifacts along the Missouri before the area was buried under the waters of the Oahe Reservoir.

Mort was one of a dozen students who joined the permanent crew of four. They worked from sunrise to sunset starting the week school let out in May and continuing until Labor Day. Professor Johnson and his crew worked as long on weekends in the fall and spring.

Even when it rained they worked, staying in tents on the flat bank near the main channel of the river, labelling artifacts, recording them in journals, packing them in boxes, shipping them for storage in Folsom Hall at the University.

As hard as they worked they were still able to collect only a portion of what they found. What they discovered astonished everyone. The river's alluvial plain, replenished each spring by the annual floods, had been home to an array of people for longer than anyone had suspected. Each group had left behind its own contribution to this collection.

Dragging a rake along any ten-foot stretch of the surface between the river and the sand bluffs yielded enough materials to keep one collector busy for an hour. Digging in the same area yielded a similar richness of objects older, Professor Johnson estimated, at the rate of three inches per hundred years. Objects collected at five feet might have been left as much as two thousand years earlier.

The artifacts did not stop at five feet. Down they went, as far as anyone dug. The expedition lacked the equipment to recover them intact. Professor Johnson made several trips to Pierre to plead with the Appropriations Committee for funds. He got only "maybes" and delays.

The last time he sent Mort. Mort received many "I'm sorry"s and "I wish I could"s, but no more assistance than Professor Johnson.

His return trip took him by the dam construction site. He counted eighty men working in one small area. The dam was rising overnight. It towered over the land. The money the expedition needed seemed to be committed to completing the project as quickly as possible.

Even nature did not favor the expedition. The second year a wet spring followed a snowy winter. At the end of the first week in June the river was still flooded. It reached the base of the sand bluffs, showed no signs of receding.

In tents, set on the land above the bluffs, all the objects had been labelled, recorded, boxed, and shipped off to the third floor of Folsom Hall.

The rain continued. The river kept rising. The crew sat around, waiting. Groups drove along the river, hoping to find plateaus untouched by the water.

By himself Mort climbed down the bluffs. Wearing waders he walked back and forth at the base. The flood plain had yielded such a treasure of objects the expedition had ignored the treasures of the bluffs themselves—the paintings scratched in the soft stone of the cliffs.

Mort was amazed by what he found. Paintings covered the

walls of the bluffs as high as a person could reach. The best preserved were in natural indentations or small caves. Even where they were exposed, the paintings, though worn, were still identifiable.

At first Mort saw only the subjects. The style, he noticed, was simple. Line drawings of fish, buffalo, people—all stick figures. Even in this simplicity there was an elegance.

There didn't seem to be a dramatic event the drawings focused on. What was their purpose, he wondered? Were they meant to show things as they were? To represent the daily lives of the people who lived there? Were they hopes and wishes—a buffalo drawn in a time of hunger? Or meant as thanks—drawn after the animal was caught and eaten? Who in the tribe drew them? Was one person singled out as an artist? Was being an artist an honor in such a society? Or was it simply one more job, like being a warrior or hunter? Did only men do it? Women too? The well or the lame? Or was it a group endeavor?

He looked for individual signatures, found none.

The more he studied the paintings, the more he noticed differences between them. None were fancy or ornate, but some were simpler, cruder, just as in drawings by children the age and sophistication of the child is obvious. These might indicate a different artist, he speculated, but were more likely a function of time. Some of the drawings—like the artifacts found deeper than five feet underground—must be evidence of cultures much older than expected.

Professor Johnson provided Mort with a camera, instructed him to photograph as many of the paintings as he could.

Mort lacked the knowledge to make conjectures about the dates of the paintings. He knew that the simplest of them seemed older than the others. In one short stretch he identified four distinct styles. He discovered a fifth, simpler than the others, in a small cave, its opening obscured by a bush; he had looked at it a hundred times before seeing it.

Mort grew to love the paintings. In them he saw a progression of human beings who had lived there. Like most people in the history of the earth they had hunted, eaten, reproduced, and died. He saw in their drawings the simplicity of their lives, and the beauty of that simplicity—the fish, the buffalo, the stick figure. This was their universe. As best they could they accepted it and were at peace in it. Some of them had lived longer ago than anyone had realized and had left a record of their existence more beautifully than anyone would have thought possible. Now they were gone.

Mort saw in the paintings, and in the fate of the people who made them, a symbol of a world gone awry. He became obsessed with preserving this record. He took hundreds of rolls of film. He didn't stop with photographs. He insisted that samples of the works themselves be preserved, by removing the section of bluff that included it. He had seen similar fossils, in rock, at the Museum Art School.

"In rock, yes," said Professor Johnson. "We are dealing with sandstone. It crumbles when you look at it."

Mort was not deterred. "Soon all this will be buried, and with it the evidence you need for your theories."

"The photographs will be enough."

"The work itself will be so much more convincing."

Using pickaxe and shovel, Mort set about saving a drawing of a fish and a buffalo, of the middle period, when he felt the beauty of the paintings was at its apex. He planned and worked carefully. He allowed an extra foot from each edge of the drawing. He would end up with a piece six feet wide, four feet high, in a section one foot deep. He made incisions to mark the sides. He was cutting along the bottom at a depth of six inches when the tail of the fish fell off the wall. As he removed the pickaxe, the rest of the fish and the head and front half of the bison crumbled.

Mort felt sick. He pictured the height of the dam towering

over him. He looked up, imagining one hundred feet of water above that spot.

Professor Johnson tried to persuade him that as far as anyone knew the water would preserve the sandstone drawings. At some time in the future, when they had more money and more advanced technology, they could return and remove them.

"Under one hundred feet of water?" Mort replied.

He was determined to save this record of the past. Completion of the dam had to be delayed. He filed briefs and injunctions. He made a nuisance of himself in Pierre.

His efforts produced no results. His insistence strained the bounds of civility. His friends and relatives stopped returning his calls.

Completion date was moved up to August 11.

When Mort woke on the morning of July 28, he realized the dam was going to be finished. There was nothing he could do to prevent it.

"Pictures," he told Professor Johnson when he arrived at work. "I'll take more pictures—pictures of everything." He redoubled his efforts, his aim to leave a record of anything that might be of interest.

For the next two weeks, as long as there was light. Mort photographed the paintings in the cliffs, bluffs, caves, indentations. He bought all the film in Grasslands, in Pierre, in Gettysburg. The expedition ran out of money. He used his own.

He arrived in the morning in the dark, his bag bulging with film. Even before the sun was up he started shooting. He used the zoom lens for close ups and details, wide angle lens for more general views. He didn't have time to develop the film, had no idea how well these images came out. He shot a roll, flipped it out of the camera, stuffed it in the bag, snapped in another roll. He lost track of what he was doing. He tried to reuse film that'd already been exposed. Rolls fell out of the top of the bag, lay at the base of the cliffs beneath paintings they'd recorded, waiting for the water to bury them both.

In two weeks Mort took 731 rolls of film. The expedition left them stacked in boxes in the tents, to be sent to Folsom Hall.

On the evening of August 10 Professor Johnson called together everyone who had worked on the expedition. He thanked them for their efforts, assured them that, no matter how much remained undone, what they had accomplished was not in vain. Telling them that this phase of their work was over, he disbanded the group.

Mort stayed on by himself. He brought a tent, pitched it at the base of the bluffs, and waited. On the morning of the 11th he walked across the flat plain to the river bed. The water didn't seem higher. He stuck a stick in the side to mark its level.

He spent the day at the base of the cliffs. His camera was at home. Taking more photographs seemed futile. He looked at paintings, lay in the sun, kept lifting his head to make sure the water wasn't rising toward him.

In the evening he walked back to the river. The water was no higher. That night he slept in the tent. All night he kept waking up. He imagined he heard water gurgling, looked out on the dry ground. In the morning the river level was still the same.

He spent the day at the cliffs, studying the paintings, lingering over them. He started to see them in new ways. He was surprised how many showed the river—flooded, dry, normal—and people relating to it. Occasionally he sat in front of one for hours, thinking about it, contemplating the view from that spot, studying it some more.

Each morning and evening he checked the height of the river.

For six days, its level stayed the same. Mort couldn't understand why. Maybe they hadn't closed the dam. At the last moment the governor had interceded.

He ran out of food. He drank water from the river, fished from its bank. Sitting, fishing, he grew to appreciate the river even more. He heard voices in it—talking, singing, laughing—as it flowed along, voices from other peoples, other times.

He fished only to eat, quickly caught what he needed—perch, bass, walleye, catfish, pike.

Once he hooked something enormous. He pulled and cranked, couldn't move it toward him, let out line, tried again. It didn't budge. He strained as hard as he could. The line snapped. Its nylon, curling and jerking like a snake, disappeared into the water.

One night he left the baited hook on land, three feet from the water. In the morning he found a catfish attached, flipping back and forth beside it.

On clear nights he slept outside the tent. He lay on his back, watching the stars revolve around the sky. One night he saw six burst from nowhere, streak to a sudden end. He heard owls, coyotes, early geese.

During an afternoon thundershower, he sat on higher ground in a small cave, watching water pour down in front of him. Behind him he discovered charred logs, bones, remnants of early fires.

On the fourth day, he decided he wanted to paint on the walls, to leave a record of his stay. He found a clean stretch, tried his knife, rejected it for a sharp stone that left broad marks in the walls. He sat in front of the bluff, uncertain what to draw. It took him two days to decide.

At first he chose simple scenes—the sun shining, a stick figure fishing, eating, sleeping, as if that might depict how calm and happy he felt. He was surprised how difficult even the simplest representation was, how long it took, how crude his efforts looked compared to the graceful figures beside them. He worked slowly. He tried for pleasing lines, graceful arcs. His subject was himself, a stick figure fishing on the bank.

On the morning of the seventh day, the water was several inches higher than the stick. Mort did not want to believe what he saw. He raised the stick to the new height, tried to go back to his drawings. All day he kept looking toward the river, expecting to see water rushing toward him. By three o'clock he could wait no longer. The stick was as far under water as it had been that morning. He saw on the bank how much the water had risen.

It continued to rise steadily. In three days it overflowed the bank, raced toward the bluffs yards at a time.

Mort now knew what he wanted to represent with his sketches: this event, in the moments before the paintings themselves were submerged. For this he needed a large, unbroken space. He searched hours before he found it.

He worked until he could no longer see, slept on higher ground on the floor of a cave, thought he heard water lapping. Several times he rolled over. Without opening his eyes he tapped with his hand. The ground beside him was dry.

He had a vision and so little time to realize it. He wanted to show these cliffs with the water rising to cover the paintings. He didn't know how to depict that. One way was to show a fish nibbling at the picture of the picture, the wavy line of the water's surface above it.

For the first time he understood that other paintings he'd seen also depicted floods rising on the walls. He hoped that if those floods had, in time, subsided, this one might too, to reveal at the bottom this record of its beginning.

Hungry, he took his pole, waded toward the channel. He saw shapes darting through the murky brown water, exploring their growing terrain. Standing at the edge of the channel, the water above his knees, he surveyed the beginnings of the reservoir. It spread out on all sides, the boundary of the channel still marked by darker water.

He caught a small perch, waded back with it to the shrinking patch of land. There he skinned and cleaned it. All the driftwood he'd gathered had floated off. With no way to cook, he sucked the juices from the fish, ate the flesh raw.

The water was ten feet from the base of the bluffs. In a day it would reach the bottom, in another cover the floor of the cave.

He tried to focus on his drawing, to shut out thoughts of everything else—how far it was from what others had done or what he wanted to show. He would finish what he could.

The stone he scratched with broke in half. He couldn't find another—all the loose rocks were submerged. He worked on with the larger half. It was harder to use. Every few minutes his hand cramped. He had to stop, hold his fingers open until the tendon stopped throbbing.

At two in the afternoon he was startled by a voice. "Mort!" He stopped, listened. Nothing else. He hadn't heard or seen another human being in two weeks. Maybe he'd only imagined it.

"Mort!" it called again.

He waded out of the cave into water that ten feet from the bluffs was half way to his knees, squinted up at a shape in a trooper's uniform peering down at him. It was Knute Svenson, older brother of Curt that Mort had gone to school with.

"How're you doing?"

Mort nodded. "Okay." His voice sounded scratchy.

"Nice bathtub you got." Knute pointed out at the water.

Mort turned, looked. He couldn't see across.

"You almost done washing your back?"

Mort stared up at him.

"You coming out soon?"

Mort didn't answer.

Knute looked down at the water. "It'd make me a lot happier if I didn't have to come down for you."

"A day or two." Mort's voice was little more than a whisper. He coughed, spoke louder. "I'm almost done."

"Can you make it tomorrow? Water's rising a foot a day at the dam."

Mort looked at the cave, the outer edge of its floor already wet. He nodded up at Knute. "Tomorrow."

"I've got a rope ladder up here. Want me to leave it?"

CLIFF PAINTINGS

Mort shook his head.

"See you in the morning." Knute's shape and voice disappeared.

Mort couldn't tell if he heard a car start.

He was surrounded again by silence, broken only by a gentle lapping against the bluffs. Beside him he heard a splash, looked down to see a fin disappearing.

He spent the night squatting in the inside corner of the cave, wondering if there was any more of what he'd seen or felt he could scratch into the bluff. In the first light he waded forward to add his final touch: a stick figure painting the flood in a cave while water covered his feet.

A BRACELET OF BRIGHT HAIR

1957

The summer she was fourteen Mavis spent at church work camp in the scruffy pine woods in the upper section of Michigan's lower peninsula. At night she joined the other teenagers eating, singing, playing games, and, when she could, sneaking off to the darkened corners of the grounds to neck with Ricky Smith, a fifteen-year-old she'd met the first day of camp. During the day her unit, consisting of four uninteresting fourteen-year-old boys and three other girls, worked with their counselor, Roderick Taylor, a student from Michigan State, on various projects. They painted all the cabins at the camp. They cleared an overgrown field. They cleaned up the beach at the pond.

One Wednesday they piled into the camp station wagon for the trip to a house that had been willed to the church, and had stood boarded up since the owners, two maiden sisters, had died. They drove down a country road that was no more than a strip of pavement between walls of woods, turned onto one with the yellow line in the middle making a lane too small for the station wagon to fit into, from there onto a road too small to have a line.

They stopped at a clearing that broke the long stretch of cool and fragrant pines, waited while Roderick read the name on the mailbox, faded and pushed backwards off its post.

"Chadwick," he announced, after squinting at it. "This is it."

"Kind of off by itself, isn't it?" one of the girls said as they stepped out into the silence.

The house was white, they guessed, or had been, what they could see of it through the trees crowding in from the sides, the bushes grown up in front, the grass waist high in the yard.

"You can tell old people lived here," Mavis said, pointing at the lace curtains in the second-floor windows, an overgrown bed of perennials on the side.

They unloaded brooms and a few boxes, carried them onto a porch so surrounded by bushes they hadn't seen it from the road.

"Watch out for hornets," one boy said, ducking, as they climbed the steps.

"Our job is to save anything there might be left of value," Roderick said as he put the key into the lock. "And then to clean. I don't think that'll take too long."

As soon as he opened the door, and the summer light and warm air rushed into the cool, dark house, it was clear much more was involved than simply packing a few items. Nothing had been touched, it appeared, since the two ladies had died. Dishes stood in the rack at the sink. The table looked as if it were about to be set. The beds were freshly made. New towels were in the bathroom. All clean when laid out, and still clean, except for the dust that had filtered into the house and settled on them.

Roderick seemed overwhelmed. "That wasn't what they told me," he kept saying, as they found more and more to do.

"Where do we start?" one of them asked.

"Just a minute," he said, "just a minute. Let me see how much more there is."

They walked from room to room, marveling at the preserved lives of two old people.

"Look at the big wooden radio."

"Does it still work, do you think?"

"And the wind-up phonograph."

"Victrola. That's what it was. See, it even says so. With the speaker."

"We may as well go ahead and start packing," Roderick decided after he'd toured the first floor. "The cleaning can wait. Goodness knows how long just that will take."

He brought in the rest of the empty boxes. "Put the stuff in them," he said. "As much as'll fit."

"Are we coming back tomorrow?" one of the girls asked.

"I don't know. We're not going to get it all done today. We'll just have to do what we can."

All day they stacked and boxed objects they felt were of value. Whenever Mavis had a moment she explored, opening doors, drawers, never knowing what she might find.

She opened the door to a closet. Clean, ironed linen—sheets, towels, table cloths, napkins—lined the shelves, smelling like dried roses.

Everywhere they went in the house it was as if the occupants had just stepped out and might at any moment return. Waiting on the sideboy were settings for two, each with a water goblet and silver, with a napkin on each plate. Beside them stood a vase of now dried flowers—a bouquet of black-eyed Susans, Queen Anne's lace, cattails, tall late summer grasses.

"Where do you think they were sitting when they died?"

"They didn't die here," Elaine said. "They went to the hospital and never came back. Roderick said so!"

On the first floor they worked as a group. Mavis got all the high jobs—clearing off the top shelves, taking down curtains. She'd grown so quickly she felt like a baby giraffe, with legs and arms wobbling out all over—and long blond hair that no matter what she did with it didn't seem right. Finally she'd bound it in one long braid that at least kept it out of things.

They started in the living room, cleaning, sorting, putting items into boxes—books, a family Bible, "Joseph and Helen Chadwick" inscribed in front, and, below that, "Beloved Daughters Mary and Edith." Photos of them—together in some, separate in others—one short, dark, serious, the other blond, her hair various lengths and styles. Young. Middle-aged. Old. With other people they tried to guess at: a brother, their parents; the blond with a young man, both of them smiling; a stern-looking minister.

They laughed at the old styles.

"Don't you think she's pretty?" Mavis was holding a picture of the blond one, young, teasing the boys.

"She's so old fashioned."

"She must've been. Look at her hair." Braided, and pulled over one shoulder.

"Edith," it said on the back. "Summer, 1895."

Sixty years earlier. Mavis tried to picture Edith's life, isolated in the country. Did they have cars then? She didn't think so. What about electricity? Running water? Radios? TV? And never getting married, never seeing anyone other than her own sister? She couldn't imagine it.

Many items they found were of obvious value: a tea set, Christmas plates, old candlesticks, the entire contents of a glass fronted case. These they packed separately and labeled: "The Chadwick house"—whatever the item was—"of value."

The paintings on the wall didn't seem to have much merit. Most were in a classical style, with black lines and dark tones. "A Visit From The Muse" was one, featuring a man dressed like an English gentleman and, appearing above, a demure young woman in white with flowing blond hair. "Lake Michigan At Sunset" was another. "The Boys Come Home" was a third, showing tired but unwounded soldiers marching in out-of-date uniforms behind a small band.

The backs of the books were so dusty they had to wipe them

off before they could read the titles. A few were of interest. A cookbook from 1890 that gave instructions in the running of the household and the care and treatment of servants. A social history of the town. Mavis found a picture of the Ephraim Clark residence—that house, recently painted—and a description of the early inhabitants. There was a 1903 edition of the *Encyclopaedia Britannica*. But one whole shelf was devoted to the romantic novels of Mary Phelan, and there were other titles like *Remembrances of Britain's Royal Family, By A Maid*.

The dining room also contained items of great value—the china, the silver, the table linen, the curtains—and others that seemed commonplace—plant bowls, an ashtray souvenir of Niagara Falls, another from Toledo, Ohio, some cheap cups.

The kitchen had mostly practical items, including sturdy utensils and decorative cannisters that have since come into vogue but then only seemed old.

Everything they packed and labeled so the church could use the house as it wished.

In the afternoon, on the second floor, they divided up into smaller groups.

Mavis worked by herself in a small bedroom. It contained only a metal bed, a brown wooden desk with a brown-shaded lamp on it, a molded wooden chair, and, on the wall, a dark rectangular mirror with spirals carved into the frame.

She unlocked the desk with the key which was in it, looked through the drawers.

The double drawer was full of letters addressed to Edith Chadwick, neatly bound in packets. The largest packet was from Denholm Chadwick, who must have been her brother. Mavis looked at some, but they were all cautions and admonitions, reminders to this and that, whole paragraphs of "never fears."

She skimmed through the others. There was an intense correspondence with cousin Caroline over a period of several years. Then Caroline married an older man who wasn't terribly good to her—against, it was clear from one letter, Edith's strong objections—moved west, and the letters ceased.

Double bound in pink ribbon was a packet, all in a man's hand, from one Robert Packer, addressed to "Miss Edith Chadwick." The letters she looked at said little, but a strong passion was evident in each. "My ardent love" was one phrase he was fond of. "My meadowlark," "My charming bird," "My dove" were greetings he started with. "Yours evermore," "Yours in Love," "Till We Two Are One" were phrases he ended with.

The letters, in chronological order, spanned several years—1894, 1895, 96, 97. One contained a locket of his golden hair, "Trimmed for the service of Our Country," and sent "that you might remember me as I have been." Several visits were alluded to. "Our upcoming Union." "Be patient." "When this skirmish is over." "Make me the man worthy of you."

The last, dated May 14, 1898, concluded with "but a short time more," and was signed, "With undying devotion, Yours in Love and Harmony."

After that, nothing more.

Mavis sat, holding the final letter, thinking of the life of Edith Chadwick.

The light had changed. Late afternoon shadows angled across the room.

She wondered how long she'd been there, if they'd abandoned her. She listened, heard laughter from another part of the house.

She rebound the letters in pink ribbon, hoping to make them look untouched. Reaching to put the packet away, she was startled to feel, below where it had been, something soft. She pulled out of the drawer a tightly wound braid of blond hair, long enough to reach from her shoulders to her waist, and neatly snipped across at the top.

When she lifted the braid into the light she stopped. She stood, held it beside her face, examined it in the mirror. The braid was exactly the color of her hair. It could have been cut that morning from her head.

She heard voices in the hall, approaching. She put the braid and letters back into the drawer, locked the desk, and flung the key out the open window into the overgrown back yard.

"There's nothing in here," she said, meeting Roderick Taylor at the door. "Isn't it time to go?"

KILLING COONS

1972

The summer Ed turned ten, his father put him in charge of ridding the barn of coons. Until the previous year the farm'd never had many. Then their numbers increased and, all of a sudden, they were everywhere.

It was clear when one'd been in the barn—eggs broken, a squawk during the night, a half-eaten chicken lying in front of the door, a grain bag with a hole gnawed in the bottom.

They became bolder. One got into the cans outside the back door of the house. By the time anyone realized what the noise was and let the dogs out, the coon was gone.

They started climbing over the back gate into the barn during the day, even if someone was standing inside. If chased they scurried away, but kept peeking back over the gate, waiting for the person to leave.

Before evening chores two or three were lined up, in back, on the side, in the field off the front, as if they could hardly wait until the people were gone, and they could get at the milk and cat food set out for them.

Ed's father was disgusted. One evening he sat under a tree with the .22, waiting for them. Ed and Edna listened from the house. They heard several pings, then a thud. A long period of silence followed. Ed's father trudged in.

"Any luck?" Edna asked.

"Couple of pieces of foundation stone broken. Two bullets imbedded in the siding."

The next day his father came up to Ed with the trap when he was playing outside, set it down, said, "Here, it's all yours. I give up. Take it away."

Ed started planning.

In the evening, after chores were done, he waited, watching where they came from, the routes they followed.

At the busiest place, in front of the barn where two paths intersected, he put the trap, baiting it with peanut butter and honey, leaving the bait on the tray that triggered the sliding doors.

The next morning he hurried out to look. The doors were shut, but the trap was empty.

"You know what it is," said his father, puffing on his pipe. He'd tried without success for a week. "They take turns. One holds the door open while the other goes in and eats."

Ed used the same bait with the same result the next two nights. He and his father had an argument about it.

"It's like fishing," said his father. "You don't just plop the lure down on top of the fish. You throw it past and work it through, so it looks natural. You should move the trap to the back of the barn, near where they come in. They have noses, they'll smell the bait." He waved his pipe for emphasis. "I was talking to a couple of guys in town. One said, 'Try peanut butter sandwiches,' but two others said, 'No, fig newtons does it every time.'" He handed Ed two boxes of fig newtons.

Ed moved the trap to the back of the barn, took a section of cookies, broke it open, put one loose and the rest of the package wrapped in the back of the trap, left the sliding door near them closed, the other one open.

The next morning when he walked out he found both doors shut. A small shape huddled inside, looking out.

He ran in to tell his father. "I-I-I-I got one!" he said, smiling. "It worked."

"It's about time," his father said.

"Big or little?" asked Edna.

"Not v-v-v-very big."

"A young one?" she said.

He nodded. "What d-d-d-do I do with him?"

His father looked at him. Smoke drifted from his mouth. "What do you think you do with him?"

"L-l-l-let him go," he started to say.

"People used to. They took them to the other side of the river and released them. The theory was, they'd never swim back. But now there're so many, if we take them over there, and the people over there bring them over here . . ."

"You sh-sh-sh-shoot him?"

His father shook his head, took a puff on his pipe, held up two fingers. "Two reasons. One, it's your job, not mine. Besides, remember the last time I shot one? It blew the side out of the trap." He stopped a moment, puffed again. "I don't like shooting them." There was another pause. "It bothers me."

Ed looked toward Edna, as if she might help.

"You take the largest water tank," his father explained. "Fill it higher than the top of the trap. Twenty inches should do it. And lower the trap into it."

Ed bit his lip, looked at his father with wide eyes.

Edna spoke up. "How long does that take?"

"Not very long. It's fast enough. Fifteen, thirty seconds, a minute, I don't know." He stopped to relight his pipe. "Look, I don't like it myself. I don't like any of it. Do you have any better ideas?"

She shook her head.

"Do you want to do it yourself?"

She didn't answer.

"Then that's what he does. You know we've got to get rid of them. There isn't a chicken left in the barn." He turned toward Ed. "Okay?"

"S-s-s-suppose I let it out and sh-sh-sh-shoot it?"

His father shook his head. "Too dangerous. Suppose it got away?" He put his arm on Ed's shoulder. "It's not a job anyone likes. I did three last year. Now it's your turn."

Ed's legs felt light walking out to the barn, as if they weren't quite touching the ground.

He filled the tank, watching the patterns the jet of water made on the surface, bubbles rising when the hose nozzle slipped to the bottom. When he leaned the hose against the right edge, the water swirled around counterclockwise. When he switched it to the left side, the two directions collided and roiled, going no direction, until the water around the outside started moving in a clockwise motion.

He tried to guess how high he needed to fill it, didn't stop until the tank was overflowing. When there was no question that he had too much, he shut off the hose, walked to the back of the barn.

He squatted down, peered into the trap. The coon looked so small, huddled at one end. Ed studied him, the two separated by the crisscrossing bars. The fig newtons, even the plastic wrap they'd been in, were gone.

"Have a good meal?" he thought.

The coon reached out with its right front paw, grasped the bars. The movement startled Ed. The paw was so delicate, its grip on the metal so fine, it looked like a hand.

Ed wanted to put his hand, even a finger, out and touch the paw. He was afraid to. He thought of the diseases raccoons carry, of the danger of its bite.

He tried to connect the late-night squawks, the half-eaten chickens, all the stories he'd heard, with the small, fuzzy creature he saw in front of him. He couldn't. Still, he kept his hands squnched into his lap, and didn't move.

After a while, he talked to it. "I'm s-s-s-sorry," he said. "If you stayed out in the field . . . But when you s-s-s-start coming into the barn and eating chickens and making h-h-h-holes in the grain . . ." He wondered if the captive was large enough to do these things. He knew it was. "It h-h-has to be done. You understand."

The coon stayed in the opposite corner of the trap. If it understood, it gave no indication.

Ed stood, bit his lip again, picked the trap up by the handle. It weighed less than he expected. Holding it away from his body, he carried it to the front of the barn. By the time he reached the tank his arm hurt.

He set the trap down, thought a minute. He didn't like having the power he knew he had, didn't like what was about to happen. He looked around the empty barn. Flies buzzed in the sunlight. Everything else was still.

There was nothing else he could do.

He picked the trap up, swung it over the water, hesitated a moment, and plunged it down to the bottom.

Despite his vow, taken a moment earlier, not to look, he couldn't turn his eyes away.

As the trap descended into the water, the coon started swimming. Ed only saw the top of the trap in the tank. He knew it was swimming from the motion of the water, lapping away from the side. As the water rose up the sides, the swimming continued. Even when the water covered the trap and the trap settled onto the bottom, the gentle waves kept bobbing away from the top, a little faster, it appeared, a little more frantically. Ed took his hand away, half expecting the trap to rise from the exertions of the coon. It didn't move.

He thought about swimming. What if he were trapped with a lid over him and swam and swam but couldn't rise to the surface until his lungs felt like bursting. He tried to imagine what the coon felt, if it knew what was happening and was scared, or if it just did what it was doing whenever it was in water, swam though it didn't like to, when it wouldn't swim the river, swam as long as it had to or could.

The waves rocked out more slowly. A few small bubbles floated to the surface.

The last thing Ed saw was one of the paws reaching out at the top corner of the trap, fully extended, reaching out again. Then the claws retracted, the paw drifted down through the water, and the waves stopped rocking.

CARNY MAN
1960

Mavis ran the box office for the Thursday night performance of *A Midsummer Night's Dream*. It was held at the high school she'd graduated from two months earlier, presented by a traveling Shakespeare troupe as part of the Watervliet Arts Festival. The week ended with the county fair.

She, Cindy, and Lana talked together, waiting for the few people standing outside to go in so the show could begin.

Five minutes before the 7:30 curtain a man none of them had seen before walked up, bought one ticket.

Mavis watched him go into the auditorium. "He was interesting."

"I guess you thought so," said Cindy. Her gum snapped. "The way you looked at him."

"You didn't think he was attractive, did you?" Lana made a face.

Mavis considered. "Unusual. You don't see people like him much around here."

"Thank God," sighed Lana.

"Come on, Mavis." Cindy sucked in a bubble. "He was so old."

"He must've been fifty!" Lana made it sound ancient.
"He wasn't that old."
"He was bald!" Lana exclaimed.
"Balding."
"You know what I mean."
"Where do you think he was from?" Mavis asked. She repeated his accent. " 'One, please.' "
"Mavis has a crush! Mavis has a crush!" Lana bounced up and down.
Cindy started laughing in the middle of a bubble. It broke all over her face. That made her giggle.
"Oh, stop," Mavis said.
She looked out at the lobby. The lights blinked. The stragglers turned toward the auditorium. Cindy and Lana followed them in, still giggling.
Mavis shut the window of the ticket booth, waited in the door for last minute customers.
When the auditorium lights dimmed, she shut the ticket booth door, snuck into the back of the theatre, sat in the last row next to her two friends.
The lights came up on an empty stage. The auditorium was only a quarter full.
From the entrance of the actors, Mavis watched, enthralled. It was the first Shakespeare play she'd seen. The language was strange and hard to follow. Some of it sounded stilted, some very beautiful, even if she wasn't sure what it meant. There was something about the sets, the costumes, the lighting, the acting she found magical. She didn't take her eyes off the stage.
Beside her Cindy and Lana whispered and giggled, about boys, about what she said he said, and "did you hear . . . ?"
The balding man sat in the row in front of them, intent on the stage. Twice he turned around and glared at them.
"Shh," Mavis whispered to them after the second time. "You're bothering people."

They moved across the aisle, left at intermission.

At the end Mavis sat in her seat, staring into space, thinking about what she had just seen.

The balding man stretched, started to leave, turned, saw her sitting. He smiled. "Did you like it?

She nodded. "I'd never seen it before. What happened at the end?"

He gave a brief explanation.

She smiled. "That's what I thought. I liked the Pyramus and Thisbe part."

"Bottom was very good. The actor. I've seen him before, I can't remember where. The rest of them weren't up to him."

"Have you seen many plays before?"

"Oh, yes. Especially Shakespeare. I've seen *Dream* three or four times before."

She looked blank.

"This play."

"Oh." She smiled. "Are you associated with—" She indicated the stage.

"Oh, no. Though I might like to be."

They had reached the lobby, stopped for a moment. Both were quiet.

"Well." He smiled, bobbed his head, twiddled his fingers in a kind of good-bye, backed up a step and walked away.

Pushing the door open with his shoulder, he turned, saw her still standing there, moved his hand sideways in a wave.

A minute later Mavis walked outside, watched him stride across the parking lot toward the outskirts of town.

The next night Mavis was waiting at the gate when the fair grounds opened. She hadn't been going to go. She was tired of the fair, tired of everything in Watervliet. She had no idea where she could go that wasn't so dull, but knew there had to be somewhere.

In half an hour she'd walked through the whole fair. She didn't see the booths and displays. She already knew what they showed. She'd seen the same thing the last three years.

She walked through again.

No balding man anywhere.

She'd been sure he was with the fair. He wasn't from Watervliet. That was certain.

She stopped, looked around. The lights of the ferris wheel, turning up over the darkening town, caught her eye.

Below the fairgrounds, attached but separate, lay the traveling carny that always showed up with it.

She hadn't been to the carny in years. She didn't like it, had no reason to go.

He wouldn't be there? she wondered.

She made a face. It couldn't hurt to try.

She walked down the hill into the carny, as if descending into some form of hell, she thought. She felt assaulted by the lights, the games, the pitches, noises, prizes, and all the people jostling this way and that.

Mavis looked at the booths, fascinated but a little afraid, her eyes wide at the newness of it. The hawkers with aprons, putting coins in their pockets, handing out balls, never stopped with their patter. "Step right up. Who's next? Knock the pins down, win a beautiful stuffed bear. Three tries, only a dime. Who's next? How bout you? Want to try your luck, mister? Come on, win a bear for your girl. She deserves it." The people, eager, as if they'd never been there before, looked at each other, fished in their pockets for nickels and dimes, watched others, oohed and aahed, waiting their turns.

Mavis walked along, exhilarated.

Booth after booth she stopped, watching the people. She saw some win, some try again, others miss, drift away, saying, "I almost had it. I think they rig that one so it doesn't fall over. Did you see how it was wobbling?"

People strolled by eating candied apples and cotton candy.

It seemed as if half her senior class was there. She nodded at people she knew and kept walking. She didn't feel like talking to anyone.

She smiled at what was going on around her. People looked happy. There was a magic to the carny after all. It took their minds off Watervliet for a few minutes—and they didn't even have to leave town. That had to be good.

She looked around at the bright lights, the people, took a deep breath. The summer night was pleasant, tranquil. It felt as if it would go on forever.

At the end of the alley Mavis watched the colored lights of the ferris wheel turn up into the dark sky, dip down toward the ground, heard the riders squeal as they turned over the top, clinging to the bar.

Cindy and Lana went over the top. She recognized their giggles, smiled at the sound. She watched them descend toward the ground, looked below them as they started back up.

There the balding man stood, switching the gears, pulling the levers, watching the wheel go up and down, looking out over the line, checking his watch, pulling a lever, slowing the wheel to a stop, unfastening the bar, letting out the occupants of one seat, letting on two more, taking their tickets, fastening them in, moving the wheel to the next seat, stopping it again.

A tingle ran down her spine. He was attractive, with his thinning blond hair, wiry frame. Very attractive.

She watched until the seats were filled with new riders and the wheel spun at full speed.

She was about to turn away, when he looked up, saw her, and smiled. All his teeth showed.

She smiled back.

He raised his arm, waved her toward him.

She walked past Cindy and Lana without seeing them. They turned around to see where she was going, ran giggling away.

"Hi." He spoke loudly. He smiled again. "I didn't know if you'd make it."

"I didn't know you were here."

"I didn't tell you?"

She shook her head.

He watched the riders, checked his watch, looked back at her. "That's right." Another smile. "I guess I didn't. I just assumed everyone in whatever town this is came to the fair."

"Watervliet."

He pointed a finger at her. "Right."

He started to slow the wheel down, checked his watch. "Oops." He sped it back up, watched it turn.

"That was quite a performance, hunh? Last night?"

"Yes." She smiled. "I got the play out of the library this afternoon. I read about half."

"Do you like it?"

"It makes a lot more sense when you've seen it."

He looked again at his watch. "Excuse me."

He pulled a lever. The wheel slowed to a stop. The old group got off, a new group climbed on. He pushed the lever, started the wheel going.

"I'm Nate." He held out his hand.

"Mavis." She took his hand, shook it. She liked his grip, firm but not rough.

"I work here." He pointed at his chest.

For the first time she noticed his tee shirt, black with silver letters: "Carny Man."

He turned around to show her the back: "Life Has Its Ups And Downs."

She laughed.

He turned back. "You like it?"

She smiled. "Yeah."

He looked pleased. "I thought of it myself. Had Harry the T-Shirt Man print it."

There was that accent again, not quite a twang, not quite a drawl. She couldn't tell where it was from.

"I've got a dozen of them."

She tried to remember what he was wearing the night before, if it was a tee shirt or a shirt and tie.

He checked his watch, looked up at the wheel, out at the line, back at her. "You want to take a spin?" He pointed up at the wheel.

She shrugged. "I don't know."

He looked at the line. "Come on. I can get you on this time. On me."

She wasn't fond of the ferris wheel. By the time she got off she always felt queasy. "Ok."

"Why not, hunh?"

She nodded.

He winked at her. "See you soon."

In a few minutes she was next in line, watching "Life Has Its" as he let a couple out. She climbed on. He fastened her in by herself.

The seat swayed. She put her hand on the bar in front to steady herself. He clicked it into position, stared into her eyes, smiled, put his hand over hers on the bar, squeezed. Then he was gone, and the wheel was turning, up, over the top, back down, around, up again, her stomach hurrying to keep up.

Beneath her, the fair and the carny were a brightly lit town, bustling with people. To one side lay Watervliet. It seemed small, sleepy—a few street lights; brighter lights from Main Street; street lights more scattered until they stopped. On the other side, the flat fields of the Michigan countryside, lit at first by the fair and the town, faded into lush darkness.

Above, in contrast to the glow of the lights, the sky seemed black. Through the white haze of the fair she saw a few stars.

Mavis gripped the bar with both hands. She loved plunging toward the brightness of the fair, rising above the dim light of the town, starting down over the darkness of the fields, the whole trip controlled by the carny man with his levers.

Before she wanted the wheel was slowing. She stopped, swaying and rocking at the top, while others got off.

When he let her off, Nate smiled. "Enjoy the ride?"

"Yes!" She grabbed his arm to steady herself, jumped down beside the levers. The earth kept swaying and turning. She held onto a guy wire.

"Watch your hands." He stood beside her, pushing the lever.

Gears whirred. The wheel started turning.

"Haven't done that in a while, have you?"

She shook her head.

"Didn't think you'd like it, did you?"

"How did you know?"

"People either love it or think they hate it."

"What about you?" she asked.

"I can't stand it." He smiled a half smile.

"I liked seeing the view—the town and the countryside. Seems pretty small from up there."

He watched the wheel, checked his wrist.

"Where are you from?"

"South Dakota. Why?"

"I couldn't place the accent."

"Town smaller than this."

He checked his watch again, pulled the lever, slowed the wheel down, exchanged groups, started it again.

"You done this long?"

He shook his head. "Just took it up this spring."

He stared at the wheel. "My mother died last winter. My father retired, left me with the cafe to run. It made a living, but that was about it. Not exactly stimulating fare."

"Not like this."

He looked at her. His face broke into a smile until all his teeth showed. "Not bad." He pointed his finger at her. "I like that."

He thought a minute. "It gets pretty lonely in Grasslands by yourself."

"It does that any place, doesn't it?"

He looked at her, nodded. "That it does." He pointed his finger at her again.

"So, anyway, long about April, I said to hell with this, put a 'Gone Fishing' sign in the window, and took off, hitching. I hooked up with the carny outside New Harmony, Indiana. Early May it was. I happened on it outside of town. I walked in, asked if they needed any hands. They started me on as a grip. All gears and levers, taking down, putting up, loading and unloading.

"Then Clint, guy who runs the ferris wheel, he got drunk, broke his leg in a fight. And here I am." He pointed at his shirt: "Carny Man."

"What's it like being on the road? Is it as exciting as it seems?"

He frowned. "At first it is. But after a while it gets monotonous. Every town seems the same. You swear it's the same people from the town before. And watching the wheel—five revolutions a minute twelve hours a day—isn't exactly thrilling." He watched the wheel. "Grasslands is starting to look real good."

"Where?"

"Home. South Dakota."

She nodded, thinking.

"I might hang on a little longer. Clint's leg's about mended. I don't know."

They stood, quiet in the night air, the ferris wheel turning around and around above them. Mavis thought about what it would be like not to be in the same place every day, wondered how long it would take her to get bored.

"This is the second time I've done it. The first time, the summer after I graduated high school—I must've been about your age."

She nodded.

"I'd gotten into college, didn't have any interest in going. The fair came through Grasslands the week before I was supposed to leave. When it left, I was with it. Did the whole tour, didn't jump off til it came round again."

He thought a minute. "Guess I liked it better the first time around. It was all new to me. I didn't mind the drinking. It made me feel like a man. And the women. I didn't realize how sleazy it is."

At 10:30 Mavis looked at her watch, surprised how late it was. "I, uh, ought to be going."

"Stick around. We're done at eleven."

Mavis wagged her head from side to side.

"You like to party? Parties every night. That's all the carnies know how to do. How about it?"

She shook her head. "I don't think I should. My parents are expecting me at eleven." She wished she hadn't said that. She wanted to seem sophisticated.

"You're sure? Just this once?"

She smiled. "I think I better. Sorry."

He nodded. "What about tomorrow?"

She wasn't sure.

"I'll be here all day, from eleven in the morning, watching it go round and around."

She wanted to, didn't know if she had the money.

He fished in his pocket, pulled out a card. "Here, how 'bout it? Rest of our stay on me."

She smiled, took the pass from him. He squeezed her hand as she did. She put it in her pocket, stared at him. He stared back.

The wheel kept going around longer than it should. She pointed up at it.

He smiled. "Oops." He turned, pulled the lever toward him.

She touched his shoulder. "See you tomorrow," she whispered and walked away.

At the beginning of the alley she stopped, turned back. He was watching her. He smiled, waved. She smiled, held up her hand, moved it from side to side.

Her parents were asleep when she got home. There was a note on the kitchen table "Turn off the lights. Fluffy is out. Bring her in if you can."

She could have stayed out all night, as long as she'd gotten home before they woke up. They wouldn't have known.

She sat in the back yard at the picnic table, stroking the cat. It was a warm, caressing night. She watched the stars, trying to think. She didn't go to bed 'til after two.

At seven Mavis walked up to the entrance to the fair. She wore a skirt and jersey she thought Nate'd like, a little red lipstick and a dab of perfume. She'd told her parents she was spending the night at Cindy's.

She stopped, walked back and forth outside the gate, trying to decide whether or not to go in. She saw two people she knew approaching. She took out her pass, hurried n.

She went straight to the ferris wheel. She saw Nate before he saw her. God, he was attractive. He was standing by the levers wearing a black Carny Man tee shirt, checking his watch, the wheel, the line, then looking down the alley. He broke into a smile when he saw her.

She smiled back, waved, walked toward him.

"How you doing?" he asked when she was close enough to hear, his whole face smiling. "Have a good night?"

"Yes."

"Me too. Spent it all outside, down by the river." He pointed. "Just lying on the bank, thinking."

She watched him. "I'm glad you came to the play."

"Me too." He switched loads.

"I finished it this afternoon. I understand it now. I was confused at the end."

She stayed all evening, talking, watching him work, taking another spin on the ferris wheel, getting him a hamburger and a soda, liking him more and more, worrying what would happen the next night when the fair ended and the carny moved on.

At eleven the fair closed. People went home, leaving a mess of papers and trash on the grass. Lights shut off. The carny looked like a deserted village, shapes and shadows rising over the land. The ferris wheel seemed abandoned—empty and dark and still.

Nate and Mavis walked hand in hand into the village of campers, trailers and tents the carny people called home. He showed her the camper he was living in. "Going halves with the guy who owns it. Not much more there for me but a bunk and a place to store my gear. Don't spend much time in there—just to sleep, or get in out of the rain."

Mavis smiled, imagining lying in it with him while rain splattered on the roof.

They stopped at the party. A radio played loud country music. Six-packs were scattered all over, butts and empties strewn around, whisky bottles in every other pocket. "Everyone in a hurry to get smashed," Nate whispered to her. She liked his mouth against her ear, the closeness, the privateness among all these people.

In the corner a couple was yelling, calling each other unpleasant names. "He's going to hit her," Mavis thought. She pulled at Nate's arm, as if to urge him to prevent it.

He didn't look. "Yeah, Scott and Mary are at it again. Pretty, isn't it."

Mavis kept staring back at them, sure something horrible was about to happen. Around them people drank, smoked, kissed, talked as if they weren't there.

Nate and Mavis walked across the field, watching fireflies scoot across, up, down, blinking as they flew.

It was cooler. Mist hung over the grass. Everything seemed darker with the fair lights out.

Nate led her into a bank of trees, down a few feet. Mavis stopped. She couldn't see a thing. Nate held her hand, took a step forward.

"Hey, what the fuck!" came a voice under their feet.

Mavis jumped.

"Oops. Es occupado."

"Watch where you're going."

"Sorry. I didn't see you."

Mavis felt her heart pounding.

Nate led her back up into the field.

"What was that?"

"Guess someone else got there first."

He led her to another opening. "Stay here. I'll check it out." He disappeared into the trees.

Behind her a guitar twanged, a scratchy voice sang, people laughed and shouted, sounding drunk. Above them, the fair looked like a ghost town.

Mavis looked back at the trees Nate had disappeared into. For a moment she wondered if she'd ever see him again.

Out he popped from the opening. "All clear."

He led her between the trees. They walked down three feet. Mavis stopped. It was as dark as the first place. She was afraid to move.

"The river's five or six feet in front of us. Stream. Whatever you call it."

The air felt damp. Mavis smelled the water, heard it gurgle over rocks.

With him leading her she took a few more steps, stopped.

They sat on the sandy bank and talked, his head in her lap. She ran one hand through what was left of his hair. The other found his in the dark, intertwined her fingers in his.

She leaned over, with her hand to guide her, located his mouth, started kissing him.

They ended up making love.

All afternoon Mavis had debated whether she should or not. First she'd decided not to, if he was leaving the next day. Then she decided to, for the same reason.

By the time she got to the fair she'd decided she wouldn't.

When she first saw Nate, felt her body respond, she decided maybe she would. Whatever happened was fine.

She was glad it was so dark he couldn't see her, wished she could've seen him.

He even used a condom. It didn't fit her image of a carny man. And he didn't throw it in the stream, the way everyone said they did.

Afterwards, Mavis lay with her eyes shut, holding him to her, feeling as close to anyone as she'd ever felt. Now she could die, she decided, it'd be all right. For once in her life she'd been happy.

She must've fallen asleep. She woke up, she couldn't tell how much later. Nate was still pressed against her. Behind her she heard a country song, the laughter of drunken carnies.

"Nate?" She kissed his ear, remembering a line from the play. "Asleep, my love?"

"What, dead, my dove?" he answered, sounding half asleep.

She smiled, ran her finger around his mouth. "What time is it?"

"I don't know. Not too late. You have to leave?"

"No. I'm spending the night with you."

"Mmm." He nuzzled into her neck.

A shout filled the air.

"Do they ever stop?"

"Sometimes. They pass out or it gets light. Whatever comes first."

They were quiet. Mavis listened to the water gurgling over the rocks, her eyes wide open. She saw nothing.

She played with his hair. "How old are you?"

"Forty."

"Oooh, you're ancient." She tried to sound like Lana. "I'm seventeen. I think that's illegal." She giggled, stopped, kissed him again.

"It's been done before," he said.

"Are you married?"
"No."
"Free?"
"There's not a lot to choose from in Grasslands."
She played with his hair. "Me too."
"Mmm?"
"Free."
"No, you're not. You're chère."
"What?"
"Dear. Cherished. It's a bad joke."
"Oh." She held him against her, thinking. "Where's the carny go next?"
"I don't know. Not too far."
"Dowagiec?"
"Something like that."
She tried to see the answer to her next question in the darkness above her. "Would it bother you if I came with you?"
"Oh, no, no, no. You don't want to do that."
She pulled away from him, sat up. "That's what I thought."
"What? what are you talking about?"
"You're just like everybody else. How many times have you done that before? You act so kind and considerate. You even use a condom. Huh." She snorted. "You're a carny man just like everyone else." She moved away from him.
He tried to hold her.
"Let go of me."
"Mavis, wait."
"At least I'm not pregnant. Thanks a lot."
He grabbed for her hand.
She slid away, felt around in the dark for her shoes.
"Would you listen to me."
"What?"
"Just listen."
"Yeah?" She kept patting the bank.

"I am not like that. I have not done this with anyone but you in a long time."

"Really?"

"Really."

She stopped looking for her shoes, sat, waiting for what he said next. From a camper she heard two people arguing. She wondered if it was Scott and Mary.

The argument got louder. The noise from it invaded their dark space, hung over both of them.

"That's why I don't want you to stay. It goes on all the time. Work, party, get drunk, fight, wake up, start all over the next day. You'd go out of your mind."

"You'd be there."

"Where? in half a camper, with Frank? Unshaven, snoring, drunk."

"I don't know."

"Listen." He waited. "Are you listening? You're not about to leave?"

"No." She turned her head toward his voice, hugged her knees to her.

"What if, when it left, I stayed here?"

"In Watervliet?"

"Wherever we are."

"There's nothing here."

"There's you."

They both were quiet.

"What would you do?"

"I don't know, get a job. Farm hand, carpenter. I don't care. I can do anything."

A tingle ran up the inside of her thighs. "Why?"

"I told you. I've about had it." He stopped. His voice got quieter. "And I'd like to stay with you. And just see what happens."

In the dark his hand caressed her cheek. She grabbed it, pressed it against her face.

"What do you think?"

She didn't say yes. She didn't say no. She didn't answer at all. She sat, holding his hand to her, hearing the river below them, Scott and Mary in the background, picturing the next evening, after the fair was over: the ferris wheel turning around for the last time, coming to a stop as he pushed the lever in, the colored lights going off, the sounds and smells of the fair ending. People drinking, working, fighting, as everything was dismantled. The booths, displays, even the ferris wheel itself, taken down, folded up. Until about morning, when the sun was coming up, she and Nate were left standing in the empty field, watching the carny caravan pull out through the grassy ruts, headed for Dowagiec.

HAYING
1977

Nate slipped his fingers under the twines, picked up the bale of hay. It barely bounced up and down. "Nice tight bales," he thought, "the whole field full."

He walked with the bale toward the wagon, pushed it off with his thigh, tossed it up to Ed's foot. While Ed stacked it, a bale from Mort landed by his other foot.

Marvin on the tractor seat pulled on the throttle. The wagon moved toward the next stack of bales.

Nate looked ahead. Only a few more were left in Marvin's east field. He bent, ran his hand over the fresh stubble. It was damp. Dew was already falling. He'd felt it on the last few bales.

The wagon stopped at the next pile. Nate tossed his three bales up, waited for Mort to throw up his four and the wagon to move before walking to the last pile. He was getting older, he guessed. Or maybe he was just tired. The first two loads they'd picked up, he'd run from pile to pile, stood with a bale in each hand when the wagon got there. Seven hundred bales later he wasn't moving so quickly.

Mort wasn't either, he noticed. Maybe it wasn't just old age.

Marvin had the easy job, sitting on the tractor seat, watching the three of them do the work. Of course he'd been out since ten, raking, baling, picking up, unloading off the wagon while the three of them stacked in the barn. Nate guessed he'd earned a rest.

Nate reached the last pile, sitting at the top of the hill. He took a breath, found the strength to lift the last four bales he'd ever throw up. The next night he disappeared on his boat.

Ed threw the last few bales five high onto the pile. He always stacked the wagon his way, loading it full from the front, even if the back half ended up empty. Arguing with him would't get him to change. He was strong enough the extra lifting didn't bother him. Like an ox, Nate thought. No matter how long he worked his rhythm never seemed to change.

Nate leaned against the wagon on the left side, across from Mort. Above them Ed placed the last bale in the middle on top of the pile, sat down on top of it. His red suspenders seemed to glow in the twilight.

Nate looked down the field. Usually Mavis would have walked out with Alice by now to help, after she'd shut the cafe. She wasn't in sight yet.

He stood, studying the hay dust mixed with sweat on his arms. He didn't feel like moving. To his side, even the tractor sounded tired, idling—putt putt, putt putt putt.

He stretched. He felt clean and trim, as if there was nothing excess about him. Picking up hay always did that for him. He scooped up a handful of loose hay, held it to his face. The fresh smell made him feel like smiling.

It seemed as if he'd been helping someone with hay all his life. When he was in high school he'd worked for Ed's father as a hand—haying, milking, mending fences—whatever needed doing. Later he remembered Marvin showing an interest in Gladys the first time the two of them'd gone to help Marvin's father's with the haying there.

He still looked forward to it. Not so many hands were left in town anymore. A farmer needed all the help he could get. They planned it now. Mort'd even made a chart. "Schedule for Haying Grasslands" he'd called it. Marv's place was first, he had high ground, it dried out fast, then Ed's high three, Mort's two, Ed's lower two. Only Sven Carlson wouldn't cooperate. Stubborn as the day is long, Mort called him. Nate didn't enjoy the times they'd had to go to Sven's to pick up hay after they'd finished someone else's. They ended up staying until one, two in the morning, feeling by the end more like draft horses than people.

Marvin shut off the tractor. It hadn't sounded loud—it was a noise they were used to—but the silence seemed intense.

Marvin swung down from the tractor seat, walked back, stood leaning against the back of the hay wagon.

"Nice hay," Nate offered.

Marv nodded. "Got supper and some brew back to the house."

"It can wait." Mort scratched his forehead, lifted his feed cap, ran his hand through his sweaty hair.

It had gotten to be a ritual, on the last load of the day, lingering in the field, instead of hurrying in.

A warm breeze blew up the field, tickled their nostrils.

"Gonna be hot again tomorrow," Mort observed.

"One more field," Marv said. "You ready for it?"

Nate nodded. "Tomorrow?"

"I don't know, might give it another day."

"I was thinking about taking the boat out. It's a good time for walleye."

Marv nodded. "I'll wait."

"Anyone want to join me?"

No one answered.

"Thanks," Marv finally said. "Farmers don't have time for things like fishing."

"Ought to make some," Nate answered. "Be happier, live longer."

Marv nodded, picked at a loose splinter on the wagon floor.

"I get any extra I'll bring you some."

"Hear they're hauling sturgeon out of there too." Mort smiled over at him. "You gonna give them a try?"

Nate shrugged. "I might. Anything that exists I'm willing to go for."

Mort nodded. "Save me a couple."

Nate smiled. "Sure thing. Five or six at least."

"N-n-nice night."

Ed's voice floated down to them out of the sky.

Mort chewed on a stem of alfalfa, considered the callouses on his hand. "Gonna be dark soon."

The night settled in quickly. In a few minutes they could see little more than the wagon and some of the field around them.

"C-c-c-can you see the reservoir f-f-f-from up here?"

"Might be able to," Marv lifted his head to answer. "I don't know."

"I th-th-think I can."

"Be easier to tell in daylight. I know you can see the other side." Marv picked off the splinter, flicked it into the grass. "When you can see anything."

Nate looked around the field. A mist had settled over its lower parts, reflected white back up at them.

All that time haying, thousands and thousands of bales, he'd never done anything but pick it up. Never mowed, never teddered, raked or baled. He'd watched many times. Even in the other field the day before—clickety clickety, clickety click, the tall grasses lying down in swaths, birds flying up whose nests were in it, the meadowlarks, swooping back, trying to rescue their young, the swallows gliding around and around, diving down after bugs stirred up.

He'd meant to ask Marvin what mowing felt like. He probably had, sometime or another, couldn't remember his answer. He wondered if it gave a deeper sense of life and death, the cycle of growing, dying, being renewed. It did for him, just walking behind the tractor, picking up the baby blackbird the mower'd gotten. "There's a divinity in the fall of a sparrow," he'd thought, laying it back in the grass for its parents to find.

So much of Marvin's life was in touch with the earth, more than anyone he knew—planting, harvesting, haying, when that was done, digging graves. Like some form of jolly reaper, he thought, hearing Marvin laugh at something Mort said.

There were places you could get away from that sense of mortality, Nate felt, but haying wasn't one of them.

"I'm serious," Mort went on. "Plow up all my fields, put them in buffalo grass." Mort'd bought a pair of buffalo as an experiment the year before. Now it was all he talked about, how quickly they and their calf were growing. He was planning on buying more. "Sell off the rest of my cattle."

"Save a few, all right?" his father answered. "So you don't come running to me for food when your experiment doesn't work out."

"My 'experiment' worked for five hundred years before we were here." He thought a minute. "Just raise them the way they used to. Quit worrying about all this hay."

"What are you going to do with them in the winter? Get everyone south of here to open their fences so they can head down to Texas like they used to?"

Mort shrugged, picked at a callous.

"Gonna need a little hay, seems to me, to see them through."

"We'll see."

"Un-hunh. And when the ground's snow covered from November to March don't be coming to me when you run short. I use all I raise."

Above them the sky formed a dome speckled with stars. Nate craned his neck, checking for favorites.

Everything grew quiet. A breeze blew up from below, adding sweetness as it climbed.

"We can head back, if you all want."

"That's all right." Mort worried his callous. "No hurry."

Marvin looked at Nate. He shook his head.

They all knew that moment—when they were tired but relaxed, with the day's work done—was special, didn't want it to end.

A high-pitched noise sent chills down Nate's spine.

"C-c-c-coyotes! Hear them?" Ed called from above. "Th-th-they're t-t-t-teaching their young." He stood on top of the pile of hay, as if by being higher he might hear them better, the two red lines on his chest bright against the black sky.

Mort raised his head. "Those aren't wolves, are they? They're coming back too."

"Th-th-they are coyotes! W-w-w-we hear them every night, up b-b-behind our place."

Nate stayed as still as he could, waiting for the next ones. Mort turned his head and listened. Marvin seemed to freeze where he was.

Calls from a hill to their left answered those from a hill to their right. A chorus of yelps, yowls and whines responded from a hill behind them. All three groups repeated their noises, once, twice, a third time. The men stood like statues on their own hill, listening to the aurora borealis of sound around them.

In moments it was over. Silence surrounded them. No one moved. No one spoke.

Nate looked down over the field. The mist formed a white moat at the bottom. Through it he could just make out two shapes in silhouette walking toward them, one larger, one smaller. He watched them cross the bottom, start the slow climb up. Somehow they seemed so far away and fragile, like shadows emerging from the mist.

SHAKESPEARE BY PHONE

1978

In the day and a half after Nate disappeared, Mavis kept expecting him to show back up. As the hours went by without a word or sign, she invented more complicated explanations of what might have happened to him. She followed through scenarios that had more twists than a soap opera.

He had landed on the east shore before dawn. Exhausted, he'd slept several hours, then offered to help a farmer there pick up hay. Before he'd been able to call, one of the hands had fallen and broken his arm. Nate volunteered to drive him to the hospital in Aberdeen—in the farmer's truck—and wait for him. He hadn't called from there because the phones were out, for some reason she wasn't sure of. Or he had called and hadn't reached her because she'd been out looking for him, worried for no reason.

Or he'd run into some old friends from his carny days, gone off on a drunk with them. And of course he couldn't come back until they'd showed him their latest equipment or taken his money in a new rigged card game. Then they'd enlisted him to go back on tour with them—one of their key men had gotten hit by a camper the day before and they needed help. He wouldn't be able to return until they came back around again.

When they found his body, Mort had identified it. Mavis couldn't bring herself to look at it. Alice had, fascinated and afraid, absorbing the reality of her father's death. Mavis knew what bodies looked like after a day and a half in the water, the skin softened and swollen like an overripe grapefruit. She didn't want to see him that way. She walked toward him holding Alice's hand. A few steps away she shut her eyes, turned aside. She wanted to remember him as he had been, not as some cruel joke had transformed him.

Not seeing him made it easier to think he wasn't gone, but off on a trip he'd be back from soon.

In the beginning she thought that almost constantly. It was easier to accept than the alternative.

The ashes she'd gotten back were just a box. It could have been empty, or contained anyone's ashes, even a dog's.

When Marvin dug the hole and raised the stone, she clutched the box to her, wouldn't give it to him to bury. "Fill it back in," she told him. "He belongs in the water."

"You're sure?"

She nodded. "I'm sorry."

He shrugged. "No problem." He started shoveling dirt back in. "I needed the exercise."

Time made Nate's journey longer, decreased the chances of his coming back, unless he'd signed up for another tour on the carny, like a ferris wheel the controls were broken on, that kept spinning round and round so no one could jump off.

A month after he'd disappeared, Mavis thought of Nate's return every day, but not every minute of the day. After six months, she thought of it every other day, sometimes every third day.

After a year she still wanted him to come back, needed him to, hoped he would, but didn't dare dream it. The few times she did, when she saw him so clearly she knew he was back, the disappointment that followed hurt so much she'd have been happier if she'd never pretended.

She couldn't help herself. Sometimes for three or four days in a row she saw him, it seemed, every moment of every day. He was constantly with her, more a part of her life than the table and chairs and telephone. If she woke up in the night, there he was, in the room with her, sitting beside her on the bed. If she turned on the light, he disappeared. If she kept the light off, reached out for him, her knuckles cracked against the bed board.

He still was there. No one could convince her otherwise. Why else was he so much with her?

At night, not sleeping, she sat in bed, her eyes shut, thinking. "I know you're still here." She talked quietly, so she wouldn't scare him. "How do I get in touch with you?"

One year to the day after he'd disappeared she stayed in her apartment all day, focused on Nate. Mort and Marvin both invited her over. She declined, dedicating her day to him.

She felt he was as close, as tangible as static electricity—touch him and the air crackled—if only she knew how to reach him.

She longed to have him there again, to hear his laugh, his voice, his thoughts. To be with him again, talking, laughing, loving. She had never been half so alive as she was with him, as if only with him did all of her exist.

That evening, after the world outside her window had grown dark and she'd begun to think maybe he had forgotten her, that he never would return, she was startled by the ringing of the phone. She let it ring many times before answering it. She knew it was him. The voice on the other end pretending to ask for someone she'd never heard of didn't dissuade her. She knew Nate was still there. If he'd gotten shy, if he was afraid it'd been so long she wouldn't want to talk, that only meant it was up to her.

SHAKESPEARE BY PHONE

The rest of the evening she stared at the phone, fascinated by the thought that Nate wasn't gone but was indeed waiting at the other end, if only she knew the number.

It was after midnight when she picked up the receiver, dialed seven digits at random. On the second ring a sleepy voice answered.

"Hello?" The person was male, but it wasn't Nate. "Hello?"

Mavis gripped the receiver so hard her hand cramped.

"Hello?!"

Before she could say anything the person hung up.

She let out a long breath, felt great relief, as if she'd been on the point of committing a serious crime.

This is silly, she thought. She was only calling her husband.

More than an hour passed before she worked up the courage to try again.

This time a woman answered. "Hello?"

"Yes. Is Nate there?"

"You'll have to speak up."

"Nate. Nate Johnson. I'd like to speak to him."

"Just a minute." She called off. "Is Nate Johnson here?"

Mavis heard voices in the background.

"No. There's no one answers to that name here."

"Thank you."

"No problem, Jill. You might wanna try again later. We're just getting started."

Mavis tried another number.

"No. No Nate here."

"I'm sorry. I must have the wrong number."

"Do you have any idea what time it is?"

"I said I was sorry."

She tried again.

"What number are you calling?"

She couldn't remember. "868-3974."

"What? Oh, what a goof." He laughed. "What are you, stoned?

You know what number you reached? 324-1605." He was still laughing when he hung up.

Mavis tried three or four more numbers with the same results. Finally she fell asleep. When she opened her eyes, light was coming in the window. She was half slumped over in bed, the buzzing receiver in her hand.

Evenings after that she spent dialing numbers. She couldn't wait to eat a quick supper and start calling.

Occasionally she got a Nate, but it wasn't hers.

Once she got a man whose voice sounded like Nate's. He insisted his name was Robert Jones.

Once she reached Nate Johnson.

"Nate!" She was smiling as she talked. "I can't believe it." She laughed out loud. "I've been trying for so long."

"What's the problem, Emily? You just talked to me half an hour ago."

"Emily? This is Mavis. You are Nate, aren't you? Nate Rune Johnson?"

"I'm sorry, sugar, but my name is Nathaniel Preston Johnson, and I'm black, and from the sound of your voice you're white, and the Nate you're looking for probably is too. "

"Yes, he . . . "

"That's okay, sugar. Anyone who wants to find Nate Johnson all that much's gotta be okay in my book."

"Okay." Her voice trailed away.

What she was doing wasn't working. Weeks of dialing numbers at random and she was no closer to having Nate back, or finding someone to replace him, than she'd been when she started.

Maybe she wanted too much. She had to admit she'd never get all of him back. That was more than she could hope for. She needed to be more modest. Suppose she took back just a part of him. It'd be better than nothing.

She thought through his qualities she admired. It was hopeless, she'd never find all those in someone else. Suppose she focused on just one. Something to make her smile again. That's what was missing most from her life since he'd left—joy and laughter.

Her eye fell on *The Complete Plays of Shakespeare* on the stand by the bed. She smiled, thinking of their evenings together, how silly they'd been, how much fun they'd had, laughing until her face hurt. Nate picked a passage, read one part, held the book out for her to read the next part. Sometimes they'd gone over the same passages again and again. They used strange voices, wrapped sheets and pillow cases around them for costumes, armored themselves with pots and pans until the apartment echoed with their antics. If she could find one person who appreciated that, who for a few minutes could make her forget everything else, maybe there was hope.

She opened the volume at random, dialed, and waited.

When someone answered she started right in. She didn't expect instant recognition, but she was surprised by the ignorance and hostility of the people she reached, the speed with which they hung up.

" 'O what a noble mind is here o'erthrown.' "

"Say what?" Click.

" 'I left no ring with her. What means this lady?' "

"Same to you, shit head." Slam.

" 'Build me a willow cabin at your gate . . .' "

"Hey, Meg, we've got a pervert on the phone." The line went dead.

Occasionally the person recognized it was Shakespeare.

" 'Yet here's a spot. Out, damned spot! out, I say.' "

"What is this, a spot quiz? This isn't Mrs Hensley, is it? I can't remember what comes next. I admit it, I haven't looked at that speech since Freshman English. I guess you have to flunk me, hunh?"

Mostly, though, she got nothing: empty space, no reply at all, "Oh," a quiet hanging up.

She kept trying. She enjoyed looking through the plays, quoting famous passages, finding obscure lines. She smiled as she did, remembering the fun they'd had with these same words, thinking how Nate would respond if he answered, how happy he'd be to hear from her. She saw his mouth caress the words as he'd delivered them.

She had just said Juliet's line after meeting Romeo,

> Nurse, what is yond gentleman?
> Go ask his name.

when she realized that the person who answered hadn't grunted or hung up. She went on.

> If he be married,
> My grave is like to be my wedding bed.

She was ready to hang up at the usual silent click when the male voice at the other end replied with Romeo's line on first seeing Juliet:

> What lady's that which doth enrich the hand
> Of yonder knight?
> O she doth teach the torches to burn bright.

She stopped, stunned. She didn't know what to say. After a long silence she managed to reply again as Juliet:

> My only love sprung from my only hate!
> Too early seen unknown, and known too late!

The person at the other end jumped forward to the scene of their next meeting:

> But soft, what light through yonder window breaks?
> It is the East and Juliet is the sun.

Mavis answered:

> O Romeo, Romeo, wherefore art thou Romeo?

On they went, ranging over the entire play. Mavis loved the quality of her new friend's voice, its self-assured masculinity, its musical intonations, the meanings he gave the words. Several times after he finished there was a long pause before she remembered to go on.

When streaks of light were visible in the east, they took their leave with lines from the play:

> Parting is such sweet sorrow
> That I shall say good night till it be morrow.

Mavis hung up, exhilarated. She couldn't think of sleeping. She didn't open the cafe. She went out and skipped through the fields until the sun was high in the sky, oblivious to everything but the play being repeated in her head. She loved the sound of his voice in her memory.

She tried to imagine the person who went with the voice. First she endowed him with desirable characteristics, then tempered her enthusiasm and gave him nothing but negative attributes. For all she knew he was better suited for Capulet or Friar Lawrence than Romeo, but it hardly mattered—she was more likely to be cast as the nurse or Lady Capulet herself than as Juliet.

By afternoon Mavis spent less time reliving the previous night and more looking forward to the one to come, wondering what would be the best time to call, what other plays he knew, if she could be as silly with him as she had been with Nate, when they should stop conversing in Shakespeare and talk current English, or if that would prove disappointing, planning when they should meet, how they should arrange that.

At five after eight she sat down on her bed, put the phone on one side of her, opened the volume to *Hamlet,* lifted the receiver, and lowered her other hand to dial.

THE HOUSE AT SOUTH WEBSTER
1974

Mavis wanted to find the house in South Webster.

She and Nate left Alice with her parents in Watervliet, drove north through the lower peninsula. On the way they stopped for gas. She came back from the bathroom to find Nate looking at the map.

"What's that about?" she asked, after she'd gotten back in the car. "Are you lost?"

"Just finding out where we're going. I thought we'd come in on 306."

"No." She grabbed the map from him.

"What's that about?" he asked.

"We're doing it without a map." She folded it up. "No A-6 or B-14. By the way I remember. In here." She tapped her head, looked at him to see how he was responding.

Nate was focused on how she folded the map without following the creases. That annoyed her. She lumped it up more.

She was tired of taking trips his way—the door pocket bulging with maps, the itinerary planned out days in advance. This time they were doing it her way.

"You're sure we won't get lost?"

"So what if we do? It's a small town. Okay?"

He shrugged. "I guess. Now where?"

"Straight north until we reach South Webster."

He nodded, pulled the car onto the road. Once they were at highway speed she rolled the window down, tossed the map out.

He watched it blowing in the rear view mirror. "Okay. Your way."

She found it hard to believe they'd been together fourteen years. The time had gone quickly. It seemed like just the other day they were leaving Watervliet for the first time, headed west.

Coming back made her appreciate how much she'd changed. She looked up Lana and Cindy. Lana had moved to Indiana after her second divorce. Cindy was still in town, no happier than Mavis had been when she'd lived there. She hated to think what her life would be like if she hadn't met Nate.

There were still things though that were just hers, part of her past. The house they were looking for was one—white, with the pond across the road. And her memories of it—going swimming with her father, seeing the dead dog lying in the road.

She could have come by herself, if all she wanted was to find it. She wanted to share it too, make it one more aspect of her life that was both of theirs.

They reached South Webster, drove through town, were back in the country quickly.

"Now what?" Nate asked

She pointed backwards. "We take one of the side roads." Several had gone off to the north.

"Which one?"

"I'll see when I get there. Just drive."

He turned the car around. "Can you tell me what it is we're looking for?"

"The house in South Webster."

"Any more than that? We're in South Webster and we've already passed several houses."

"The house we came to when I was four. My father's maiden

aunts owned it."

"And . . ."

"I wanted to find it—to see what it looked like."

He raised his eyebrows.

"What does that mean?"

"I didn't say anything."

"You raised your eyebrows. What kind of comment are you making?"

"Nothing. We're doing it your way."

"That's right, we are. Without comment."

He nodded.

"Would you rather I did it myself? Left you at the library, picked you up in an hour?"

He shook his head. "I'd rather be with you."

"Okay. Then stop trying to take over."

They reached the first road. He pulled the car to the side, stopped.

"North Street," the sign said.

"What road are we looking for?"

"The one it's on."

"Does it have a name?"

"I don't know."

"You don't know!"

"Not the street address."

"How will you know if we've found it?"

"I'll know."

"When was the last time you were there?"

"Four. And again when I was five."

"And you think you'll remember it? My God, I don't remember anything from four. Besides, it must've seemed enormous."

She pointed to the right.

"I don't believe this."

"This way."

He turned the corner.

"Not too quickly."

They drove the length of the street. Before long they were in the country. One house seemed possible. He stopped outside it. She studied it, the road, looked around for a pond. The house was the right color and era, but the pond was too big, too far away.

She had him turn around, try the side streets. Nothing seemed plausible. They drove back to the main road, took the next side street to the north. Its street sign was missing.

"What about that one?" He stopped, pointed at a white house, up on the right. "I see it, from the way you describe it, as above the road, on that side."

She considered it, the road. She shook her head. "No. Where's the pond? Not at this house."

They saw nothing else on that road or the side streets off it.

"Are you sure you'll remember it? That's a long time ago."

"I'll remember it."

"What if they painted it?"

"It's white in my memory."

"And if it's yellow now?"

"It will feel right."

As they drove she talked about the house, with its screened in porch; about her great aunts, how fierce her mother thought they were; about what an event it was going there, packing the car in Watevliet, driving north for hours. "When they died, they willed it to the University of Michigan."

"There you go. You could ask someone. Or maybe there's a plaque. The university. Someone should be able to help."

She nodded, didn't say anything.

"Do you want to ask?" He slowed near a man on a lawn.

She shook her head. "Just keep going."

He looked at her. "What if they tore it down? Would that make it any harder to find?"

She stared at him. "No," she said firmly, as if to stop him from being a jerk.

She paused a moment before going on.

"There was something peaceful about it. A kind of contentment. Everyone felt it there. That's why they kept going back. I knew it even then. My two great aunts baking pies every day. Staying in my own room, on the second floor. How cool and dark it was inside. The dog, Mumbo, that belonged to William, one of the other guests, lying under the table at dinner, sitting at lunch with his head on my lap while I scratched it. Going swimming in the afternoon, coming back with my father, with his blond hair and pale skin, walking across the road, holding his hand. Barefooted, stepping high on the hot asphalt.

"One afternoon Mumbo was lying on the road in the sun. A car was stopped in the driveway with its motor running. At first I thought he was sleeping. When we got closer I saw a stream of bright blood coming from his nose, drying dark on the pavement. 'Mumbo,' I started to call. His sides didn't move. He didn't thump his tail when he heard me.

"I'd never seen anything dead before, but I knew without anyone telling me that's what he was. I kept staring at him. I felt funny. Earlier he'd sat with his head on my knee. Now he couldn't do that anymore. I looked back at him as we walked toward the house. My father squeezed my hand.

"'Someone should tell William,' I said.

"He pointed to the car idling in the driveway. 'I think someone is.'

"We went inside. When I saw my mother sitting in the living room, reading, I felt relieved. Like maybe something had happened to her too. I ran to her and hugged her, and then I started crying."

She smiled, thinking about it. "William buried him by a rock in the back yard, carved his name in the stone. I remember standing there while he chiselled, telling me what he was doing. The next year he had another dog, but it wasn't the same."

She stopped. "That's when I learned that creatures you liked could die." She touched Nate on the arm. "Life went on, but it wasn't the same." She looked out the window. "That's why I wanted to find it."

They started down a third road. Before one house, white, tall, up to the right on a curve, Nate stopped. "There it is."

Mavis studied it. "I don't think so."

"Come on, white, the pond, everything the way you said it was."

"Except it's not the right house."

"Close your eyes, try to remember."

She did, opened them, shook her head. "Not it."

"I think you don't want to find it."

She looked at him. "You know, it's a little bit like having an orgasm. I don't mind not having one, but I'm not going to tell you I had one when I didn't."

He stared at her. "You're not saying you fake them, are you?"

"You know I don't."

He nodded.

"To use an expression you're fond of, 'close but no cigar.' "

He smiled. "It looks so much like it."

She nodded. "Lots of people look like you, but they're not."

"Okay." He pointed his finger at her, drove on.

"Not so fast."

Several possible houses went by, all across from a pond. Before she could decide, they were gone. On the way back, Mavis studied them. Still Nate had driven by before she was sure.

They reached the main road. No other streets went north.

"Now what?"

She wanted to try the last road again, more slowly, stop at the ones that might be possible, get out, walk around, see if one had a rock in back with "Mumbo" on it. She considered asking him to, decided not to. He'd get stuck at the house on the curve again, would go too fast past the ones she was interested in.

Maybe she'd come back another time. With Alice, if she wanted. Or by herself.

One road went south. Nate nodded toward it. "Do you want to try it?"

She shrugged. "May as well."

Soon it was apparent this wasn't the road. They reached highway speed. She settled back, shut her eyes.

"There." Nate pointed off to the left.

Mavis opened her eyes in time to see a corner of blue gingerbread flit past.

"Aren't you glad we didn't give up?"

"You got it." Mavis pointed her finger at Nate, let her hand settle onto his arm, leaned back, re-shut her eyes. She pictured the white house her aunts owned as it had looked when she was four. She remembered walking across the road with her father, feeling the warm pavement under her bare feet, seeing Mumbo lying in the road, a trail of red running from his nose.

THE LAKE MONSTER
1977

"Alice."

Mommy was shaking me.

I rolled over on my side, pulled my legs up, tried to go on sleeping.

In my dream I was lying in our little aluminum boat with the outboard motor, my head back, looking up at the sky. Mommy and Daddy fished. The boat rocked back and forth every time the Monster nudged it with his nose.

She shook me again.

I opened my eyes.

"Get dressed."

I sat up.

"We're going out on the boat."

Outside was dark, the lights of the room reflecting off the windows.

I stood up, started getting dressed.

Mommy didn't say anything.

When I had my pants on and my shirt half buttoned she came and hugged me, her arms wrapped around me. We stayed like that a long time.

"Go on and finish dressing."

She said it so quiet and her face looked so much the same, I couldn't tell if she said it or I only imagined it.

After a minute I went back to my buttons. My cheek was wet where it'd pressed against hers.

When I finished she was still standing next to me, her eyes shut. I put my hand in hers.

Her eyes opened. "Oh, Alice! You surprised me." She stood, staring at me. "Are you ready?"

I looked down at my shoes.

She bent to tie them. "That was fast."

I nodded. I'd tried.

"Well." She stood back up. "Let's go."

The car was in the driveway. The truck wasn't there.

I started to get in.

"Get in front if you want."

"What about Daddy?"

"You don't have to worry." She took my hand. "It's gonna be all right. I know it is."

I climbed in front.

Most times Daddy was the one that said, "Let's go," or he went out and we stayed home. I couldn't remember any other time we went out, just me and her.

I sat on the seat, waiting. Mommy leaned forward, her forehead resting on the steering wheel. A long time she stayed like that. Then she sat back up, started the car, drove toward the road.

I watched the dark going by out the window, the headlights lighting the road in front. On the side I saw the light on the new grass. Beside me it was dark again. It looked different too, like it changed from green to black, it wasn't just the light.

After a while everything was grey. Before long I couldn't tell if the lights were on or not.

I wondered how the dark looked on the water, if Daddy saw

what he caught or just heard splashes and reached out with the net not knowing what he'd find.

I went out with him at night once. I didn't like it. I sat in the middle in the dark and didn't turn my reel in even when he threw my line out for me. I didn't want anything I didn't know what it was jumping out of the water and landing in my lap.

At dinner yesterday he'd said, "Come on, tiger, we're going out."

I held tight to Mommy's leg, shaking my head. "No. No."

"What are you afraid of, monsters?" He laughed. "We'll be back by midnight. Long before monster time."

"No!"

Mommy rumpled my hair. "It's all right. I'll stay here with her."

He went out without us.

Now it was morning, and we were going out without him.

Mort was outside before we stopped. Mommy looked at him. He shook his head.

"What about the inlets?"

He shook his head again.

"There are hundreds of miles of them."

"They've tried everywhere."

He came around, opened the door, got in my side. I slid over to the middle. Mommy drove.

I watched straight ahead. Above us the sky'd gotten blue. Soon the sun'd be up.

"How's she taking it?" He looked over my head.

"I haven't told her yet."

Mort nodded. "Maybe it's just as well." He put his arm around me, hugged me to him. I closed my eyes.

I was bobbing up and down in Mort's big boat. Sparkling on the waves next to it was our little boat, but Daddy wasn't in it. I called, "Daddy! Daddy!"

I looked for him on Mort's boat. I looked for him in the

water. All I saw was the sun glittering off the water and, right in the middle where I had to squint to see it, the empty boat.

We turned into the boat yard. Mommy drove slow. Mort rolled his window down, leaned out to some men standing in a group.

I watched one talk. He looked toward Mommy, back at Mort. "Sorry," was all I heard.

I looked at Mommy. She nodded.

I looked at the window, saw the top half of the man moving behind us. I saw two masts go by and the boat house. I was trying to kneel to see where it went when Mommy turned off the motor.

We got out. Mort talked to different men. There were a lot, standing around. Their radios squawked for a minute and were quiet.

Mommy and I stood waiting.

"No bell."

I listened.

"That's something."

The bell they rang when they found someone in the water, she meant. "Ring ring" it clanged when they'd laid him out on shore. "Ring ring."

Mort came back to us. He didn't say anything.

Mommy looked at him. "You think they'd find something."

"That's what no one can figure. No wind, clear sky, nothing." He was quiet a minute. "Well, Mavis. We going out?"

Mommy nodded.

He took my hand. "Let's go."

We got to his boat over the jetties.

I took my life jacket from the box by the door, stood for Mort to tie it. He had his on too, put hers on Mommy, tied it for her.

"Keep your eyes open, Alice." Mommy stared out at the lake. "If you see anything, let us know."

I kneeled in my place in back, watching white water churn

out from under the boat, spreading out behind us until it was all mixed with black water the boat hadn't bothered.

In the wind cool spray landed on my face.

I watched the water running away from the back of the boat, wondering what it was I was supposed to be looking for.

The Lake Monster, she must've meant. I hadn't ever seen him. He didn't live in the white water behind the boat, the propeller'd get him and chop him to bits. But in the black water to the side, he could be anywhere there, right beneath you, even. You never knew till he surfaced.

I watched over there. I didn't see anything.

One time I heard people talking about another monster far away. We didn't have to go to other countries for that. We had one right in our own reservoir. I knew. I even heard the noises once when I stayed on Mort's boat.

Others things too. Things nothing else could explain.

Like why did Daddy ask me about him last night?

And why did he wear a loaded pistol strapped to his chest in a holster whenever he went out? It didn't matter that Mommy said having a loaded gun on the lake was more dangerous than anything he'd ever run into, and he said something about giant sturgeon. I knew why he had it.

I knew what the Monster looked like too. He was green. If you were there when he came out of the water you'd watch till he was longer than Mort's boat three times over and higher than the mast. And when he opened his mouth fire came out.

I kept watching the black water, thinking he was swimming just underneath where I couldn't see him, watching me, playing games the way our cat did once with a mouse she brought back to her kittens that she let go but wouldn't let get away. When he was ready, he would break the surface—every time there was a swell I thought that was him, starting his rise—and keep rising straight out of the water until he hung over us, waiting to come crashing down. There was nothing we could do about it then. We didn't even have Daddy's pistol.

I kept staring at the water until it almost drew me in.

I stopped and looked away.

We were so far out you couldn't see the shore in any direction. Just the sun and sky above us, and black water all around that was so deep, Mort'd told me, you could go down and down and still not touch bottom, and so dark you couldn't see your hand right in front of your face, and so cold, he said, the temperature didn't ever change. That was where the Monster lived, waiting and watching in the dark with nothing showing, not even his eyes.

If you were there looking right at him you'd know he was there not by anything you saw but only if you heard him breathing. He'd been there since before I was born, and Daddy too, even longer than that. Maybe before people ever saw this water there was the same Monster, living at the bottom and only coming up to eat. And what did he eat but boats and the people on them.

Thinking that made me feel strange, like we were going on his property and that made him mad. I wanted to go back, be closer to shore where the water wasn't so deep and maybe he didn't come, but even if he did and you saw him you wouldn't feel so all alone.

I went and stood by where Mommy sat looking out at the water. She didn't notice.

After a bit I walked into the cabin. "Mort."

He turned his head from the wheel. "Lunch time?"

"Where's Daddy?"

"I'll tell you what. Grab a sandwich there"—he handed me one—"and dig in. And you just sit here next to me and pretend I'm your Daddy. Everything's going to be all right."

We were out all day. Before it got dark we started back. The sun'd already gone down behind the hills by the time we docked.

A few boats stayed out. I saw their lights dotted about on the water. Most of them were already in.

Mort talked with some of the men. I stood beside him. Daddy wasn't there. Neither was our boat. But the truck was.

We walked back to the car.

Mommy drove, staring straight ahead.

I couldn't see. "Why's it so dark?"

Mort reached over, turned on the lights. "Mavis, are you all right?"

She didn't say anything.

My face was warm from the sun and wind. I closed my eyes. I saw waves and the sun, then the Monster, waiting and watching just under water and not once showing through.

I opened my eyes when Mort got out. Mommy kept the motor going.

"You're sure you're all right?"

She nodded.

"Well." He shut the door, looked in the window. "I'll be ready in the morning."

We drove away. Before we turned onto our road Mommy stopped, leaning over the steering wheel. Her jaw was tight. She made a strange sound.

She was that way a long time. A car came up behind us, waited, drove around.

"Mommy."

She sat up, opened her eyes. "I'm all right." She put the car into gear. We started moving, her hands tight on the steering wheel. "I'm all right!"

Something slapped my face like a rope whipping around under a sail. I opened my eyes. I was sitting on the ground outside the car. Mommy was leaning over me.

"Alice."

It went again.

"Get up."

My eyes stayed open.

"Please." Pulling on my sleeve. "You're too big to carry."

I stood up. My head was still sleeping.

"Just a little way more."

I heard waves, smelled water.

"Where are we?"

"We're going back out."

She took my wrist, pulled me along. I tried to take my arm away. She held it tight.

"Where's Daddy?"

"We're going to find him."

We walked out toward Mort's boat, me after her on the jetty. I went slow, being careful in the dark. She got way ahead. I tried to catch up. She just got farther.

I couldn't see. I stopped. Around me everything was black. Dark water lapped at the sides next to my feet. I listened. What if it was him, his tongue going, "Lap, lap"?

"Mommy!"

"Aren't you coming?" Her voice was far ahead in the night.

"I'm scared!"

"Stop screaming. I'm coming."

She stood next to me. All behind her was blackness.

I took her hand.

"What are you doing way back here?"

"There are things in the dark."

"Nothing's in the dark. Now come on."

She led me between the lapping. Once I looked down. I didn't see him, or the water. I just heard the noise. I wasn't so afraid when she was there.

Mort's boat was bobbing up and down by the jetty. I climbed on, put my life jacket on, turned my back to her. She walked away without tying it.

I sat down at my place in the back.

We backed out, past the other boats at the dock, drove into the blackness.

The motor droned on and on.

I opened my eyes. Everything was still. Mommy was standing looking down at me, wisps of white in front of her face. Everywhere else was dark.

All I heard was the lapping of the water on the sides of the boat and, far off in the distance, a bell. I listened.

"It's the fog bell. Hear it?"

"Ring," it clanged. "Ring. Ring."

All I could see was her.

"Alice." She took me by the shirt, started pulling. "Stand up."

I stood up. She took off my life jacket.

"Climb up here." She patted the top of the railing.

I looked at her.

"Climb up there."

She looped her hand around the belt in the back of my pants.

I climbed up where she said. The water seemed closer. I couldn't see it, but I heard it, black and dark beneath me.

"I want to get down."

"I've got you."

"I'm scared."

"It's all right!"

She twisted her hand tighter in my pants.

I looked down. The water was black. I couldn't see it, but I knew. It was different from the blackness that was nothing.

"The water . . ."

"It's all right!"

With the hand that was looped in my pants she lifted me off the edge, lowered me toward the water.

"Mommy!"

The water was closer, lapping at the boat, bouncing all around. There were other sounds too, sounds that were maybe him.

"Are you a big girl?"

"Yes."

"Are you Mommy's biggest girl?"

THE LAKE MONSTER

"I'm scared!"

"I have you."

I saw the water. If I reached my hand down I'd touch it. Even not touching it I felt how cold it was; cold and black. I turned slowly around just above it, my pants pulled tight into me, going round and around like a bird.

"Mommy!"

"Alice, I want you to find your father. Find Daddy!"

Around I went, again and again, getting lower and lower. My face went into the water. Water came into my nose. I jerked away, coughing.

"Mommy! It's cold. Mommy!!"

"Alice? Where are you?"

"Here."

I turned my head, looked up. I saw her eyes coming out of the blackness.

"What are you doing down there?"

"Pull me up. Please!"

"Don't struggle. I have you."

I came up a little, stopped.

"You're so heavy."

I went down some. My leg touched water. I jerked again.

"Help me. Take my other hand."

I saw it, dangling down. I couldn't reach it.

"You have to help me. I can't hold you much longer. Climb. Can you? With your feet. Isn't the ladder there? Please. You have to help me!"

Just after my hand and foot found the ladder she let go, leaned over till she almost fell in.

"Alice!"

"Here, Mommy."

I started climbing.

At the top she hugged and squeezed so hard I thought I'd burst.

"Oh, my darling. Oh, my sweet baby."

A long time she sat, holding me tight, her heart pounding against me.

"I heard him."

"Did you?"

I nodded.

She held me till her heart was quiet, soothing with her hand.

"I saw him." She talked low in my ear. "In a land under water. It was bright and dry, his mouth moving back and forth like a fish . . ." She held me away, looked at me, hugged me harder. "People were there. Other people. And a great giant fish. All living there. In a place long ago."

Even when she stopped talking and her breathing was the same as the "lap, lap" of the water she didn't let go but held me to her.

I closed my eyes.

When I opened them it was daytime. Fog was on the water, but lifting. I could see all the boat and a little way past. Above the sky was bright blue. I sat still where I was, close in Mommy's arms, feeling her heart against me, steady and quiet, and listened.

I heard her breathing, in and out, in and out, that mixed with the water lapping on the side while the boat bobbed up and down. Before long that was the Monster breathing dry in his land under water.

The sun splashed all over the deck around us. I heard planes. When I looked up, I couldn't see any.

Somewhere, out over the water, I heard voices, calling back and forth, and far off in the distance I just made out a faint "Ring ring," "ring ring."

ARTIFACTS
1984

"This still right?" I leaned over the steering wheel, peering through the windshield.

The road'd narrowed. Couldn't hardly see diddely.

"Knew I shoulda fixed the headlight. Hunh. Ed! Hey. You awake? Whoa. Jesus Christ. Look at the goddamn fog."

I wiped the windshield where my breath steamed it up.

In a dip, all I saw was white.

I stopped, started again. At the bottom, a tree, the trunk two feet across, jumped out just to the side like a rabbit, disappeared behind us.

"Damn." Didn't know this area at all. Little to the south was more my territory.

We hit a bump. I didn't see it till we were on it. Even at 10 mph the truck left the road, bonked back down.

"Oh, shit. Sorry 'bout that."

We rumbled louder.

"Another one of them and the muffler's gone for sure."

I listened. Couldn't tell if it wasn't dragging already.

Few drops splattered on the windshield. Wished it'd go ahead and rain and lift the fog. Anything but this. Cool off, turn to snow. Warm October nights were the worst. Rather a blizzard over this. Least you'd know you couldn't go nowhere.

The motor backfired, sputtered. That last bump'd really done it for the muffler.

"Oh, boy." I hit the brake. Straight in front of where the road'd been was a boulder. Roads went either side.

"Ed. Ed. You stupid retard. Wake up."

In the light reflected from the fog I could just see him slumped against the door, his head on the window.

I reached over, shook his shoulder.

"Hey. Wake up!"

I whistled, piercing, shrill.

He sat up. "Y-y-yeah?"

"Wake up."

"W-w-who's that, B-b-billy?"

"Dwayne."

"D-D-D-Dwayne?"

"Yeah. You drunk?"

"W-w-where are we?"

"You tell me. We're in my truck." I gunned it. "Needs a muffler, hunh," I shouted over the noise.

"S-s-sounds like, yeah."

"Which way?"

"You g-g-got any b-b-booze?"

"Only what's left."

I handed him the bottle. Couldn't'a been half an inch in it. "It's all yours."

"Th-th-that's it?"

"We took care of the rest already."

He slugged it down, started coughing. "Cheap sh-sh-shit."

"Yeah, you help me now, we both be in C.C."

I could see him lean forward, elbows on his thighs, staring ahead.

"Hey, D-D-Dwayne."

"Yeah?"

"You b-b-better not g-g-go no further. There's a r-r-rock in the way."

"No shit. So what do I do?"

"I d-d-don' know. T-t-turn." He started giggling and hee-ing like some kind of strange animal; ended up coughing, doubled up, leaning forward.

I waited til he stopped. "Which way?"

"How the h-h-hell do I-I-I know?"

"You're the one who got us here."

"Wh-wh-when'd I do that?"

"If you were born with brains you lost them. Listen, we were at the auction, remember that?"

"Wh-wh-when's that?"

"Tonight, jerk head."

"Y-y-yeah."

" 'Y-y-yeah.' And we were talking. And I got us a bottle. And here we are."

"Wh-wh-what were we t-t-talking about?"

"You're not just stupid, you're dumb too. I brought up the subject of the ancestorial burial grounds you was telling me about once, that your grandpappy told you about, that had old doodads lying all over the place, left from when people was buried there. Remember? I said, what do you say you take me up there, I'd like to have me a look. And we took the bottle, and that's where we are, somewhere between the auction and there. Only you gotta tell me which way to turn, 'cause I don't know where the hell I am."

"Th-th-this the road from th-th-the auction?"

"The road off the road from the auction. It's been maybe five miles since we left the highway."

"Th-th-that the f-f-first f-f-fork?"

"First rock, first fork, first knife."

"T-t-take a right."

I revved the old green beauty, took a right.

"You t-t-turn on the heat?"

"Must be fifty out."

"I'm c-c-cold."

He hunched over.

After a few hundred yards the road narrowed to one lane.

Bump bump bump, the muffler dragged on the ridge in the middle.

I leaned forward, squinting through the fog. Even 5 mph seemed too fast. One stretch was all puddles. Slippery on top. Sunk down, one, two inches. Not deep though. Had a solid bed.

"You sure this is it?"

"Th-th-this is the one."

"How you know? your eyes are shut."

"I know."

"Bet you haven't never been here neither."

His eyes stayed shut. "I know."

Damn retard. Turn him loose blindfolded in Pierre he'd still find his way there. No brains to get in his way.

I reached in my jacket pocket, pulled out a crumpled pack. "Light me a cigarette."

He reached to push the lighter in.

"Doesn't work."

"You g-g-got any matches?"

"There was a book with them." I reached in my pocket. "Must've fell out."

He patted around on the seat, found the flashlight, lit it, shone it over the seat.

I glanced down. "There they are. Back in the crack."

I switched the blower to defrost. "Hey, don't breathe so much. We're fogging up."

I wiped the windshield off, opened my window an inch. Mist covered the windshield.

I turned the wipers on. Zwit, bang, zwit, bang.

"C-c-can't you s-s-slow them down?"
"Low speed doesn't work."
"They're g-g-giving me a h-h-headache."
A match scratched. The cab lit up with an orange glow. He lit one, handed it to me. The cab filled up with smoke.
"You crack your window?"
"I'm c-c-cold."
"I can't see."
Putt putt putt putt. The motor sounded louder. There was a dragging sound underneath. The right rear wheel went over a bump. The dragging noise stopped.
"There goes the muffler."
"Wh-wh-what?"
I jerked my thumb toward the back window. The rumble from the exhaust was quieter than the dragging.
The road was no more than two tire paths with a grassy mound between. Puddles dotted the wheel tracks. The bumps got more frequent, larger.
I gripped the wheel, leaned forward. Smoke tickled my nose.
"Another five, six miles of this?"
"N-n-not too much more."
I looked over at him. He sat, head back.
"How's things?"
"Hunh?"
"Nothing."
The road dipped, started to climb. It dipped again, climbed some more.
"Less fog when we climb."
"Mmm." His eyes were shut. "'Don't b-b-bury me in f-f-fog.'"
"What's that?"
"What the old I-I-Indians say."
"Oh. What's it mean?"
"The h-h-high ground. The p-p-places they think are

s-s-sacred. In the Hills. R-r-round here, d-d-don't think they cared. By the river was as g-g-good as any. B-b-better, if that's all there was."

I started coughing, leaned forward, racking away.

"Damn." I opened the window, spat out, sat back. "Got to give up smoking." I looked at him. "Tomorrow." I slapped my knee, laughed.

What was left of the road went down a long steady incline, started back up, and stopped.

"This it?"

"The r-r-rest on foot."

"How much farther?"

"Not t-t-too long."

"Up hill or down?"

He shrugged. "M-m-mostly down."

I killed the lights, switched off the key. The rumble stopped. I smiled at the silence, grabbed the flashlight, pulled back on the handle, leaned my shoulder into the door. It creaked, the metal twanged, and it opened.

I got out, slammed the door shut, flicked my butt off into the wet grass, stood, listening to the silence.

Up on a ridge I heard an owl.

I looked around. It was one dark night. Without the light I couldn't see my hand on the side of the truck.

I moved toward the back of the truck. I felt like—what was it, one of those animals that was blind, got where it was going by feeling.

Damp night. It wasn't raining, but you moved you got wet.

I reached in the bed for the shovels, pickaxe.

"Hey, sleepy, you coming?"

The right door opened. The light from the cab lit up a white square around the truck. The door shut. Everything went black.

I heard a familiar sound. "Hey, what you doing?"

"T-t-taking a tinkle."

"You give me a hand here?"

"In a m-m-minute."

I leaned my forearms on the sides, waiting.

"Wh-wh-what?" Ed spoke in the darkness.

"I didn't say anything," I was about to say. He went on.

"Th-th-that you, P-P-Pappy? J-j-j-just come for a visit. He's a f-f-friend."

The owl boomed, closer.

The cab door opened, the square of white again around the truck.

Ed got in, shut the door.

"Hey, Ed, what're you doing?"

"G-g-going back."

"We came this far . . ."

"We're g-g-going back. You can't see it. P-P-Pappy said so."

"Ed, that was no dead spirit of nobody's grandfather. It's an owl. Hear it?"

The door stayed shut.

"Oh, come on. We didn't come all this far just to sit in the cab."

I stood, waiting.

The owl on a ridge to the left boomed, one below to the right answered.

"Christ, they're all over."

I closed my eyes. I couldn't get over how mild it was. Hadda change soon. Last year the ground was frozen by Halloween. That was different. Wouldn't 'a been out digging in that.

I opened my eyes. Mist blew in my face. Ahead, over the hill, I heard the gurgling of a stream.

I walked back to the cab, hand guiding me along the side, yanked on the door to open it, climbed back in, pulled the door shut.

We sat for a while.

"So, Ed, what's the problem? Owls don't want me messing around up here?"

He sat hunched into himself, leaning against the door. The sound of his breathing showed where he was.

"You'n me go way back. It's not like I'm a stranger. I grew up out here myself. I'm a local boy too."

Silence.

"You couldn't describe how to get there, or kind of point me in the direction?"

No answer.

"Hey, Ed, did I tell you what the fellow I was talking to the other day said? the reason I brung it up at all? I didn't think I did. Listen to this. I was down to Sioux Falls the other day on business."

"What k-k-kinda business?"

His voice startled me.

"D-d-deer?"

"You know me."

"Yeah. I g-g-guided for you t-t-two years ago. T-t-twenty-f-f-five dollars you owe me."

"I paid you."

"N-n-not the last t-t-twenty-five."

"The two bottles I give you."

"T-t-twenty-five!"

"Arright. Easy. When we get back, I got it for you, no problem. Only don't forget to remind me."

"H-h-how'd you do?"

"Hunh?"

"The d-d-deer."

"Not good. Even jacking didn't get but a few. And the thing I can't figure, price is down too. Usually, you get a scarcity, price goes up, right?"

"S-s-s-same for calves."

"Not this time."

"M-m-must be getting 'em some place else."

"Must be. So anyhow, I stopped in over at Mike's, had me a few before I left, see what was going on. And this guy there was saying, you know those, what're they called—shards, you were telling me about, and them little crockery pieces they buried the dead with. Fellow there was telling me, they're getting one hundred dollars for them over in the Twins, not whole ones either, just pieces. And those crockery thingies, there's some collector down there that's buying them up, if they're whole—five hundred bucks, just for one of them. And you know, every one I get, that's a hundred dollars in your pocket. The way you were talking, must be a fortune of them out here. I didn't think anybody'd miss them. I mean, not much they can do now for the dead, but they sure can help the living—ain't that right?"

I patted around til I found the cigarettes. Only a few left. Took one out, found the matches, lit it, inhaled, blew the smoke out my nose, cracked the window, sat back, waiting.

"One hundred d-d-dollars?"

"Yeah, well, you know, I got the contacts, I'm the one gotta truck on down to the Twins—going public, as it were."

"One-s-s-seventy-five."

"I couldn't go that high. I got gas to pay for, repairs and upkeep on the old vehicle." I patted the seat beside me. "Not to mention motel room and meals if I stay over. It adds up." I considered. "One-thirty-five."

"One-f-f-fifty."

"Done deal."

"I'm n-n-not sure."

I waited. "You know. I wasn't going to say anything. I was going to save it for the return trip. But I got a pint of "7" right here in my jacket pocket—case you want a nip now."

I reached in the left pocket, pulled it out, held it out in the air in the middle of the cab where I knew his hand would be.

I heard him crack the seal, take a few slugs.

I leaned my shoulder into it, pushed open the door. I squinted at the light, got out. The darkness when I shut it seemed like home.

I stood by the cab. I heard water lapping. "There a lake nearby?"

Silence.

I listened.

"Sounds like Pappy turned in." I waited. "I'm ready when you are."

My left hand on the side guided me to the back. I clanked out a shovel and the pickaxe, swung them over my shoulder, picked up the canvas bag. I faced backwards, sitting on the rear bumper, the tools resting on the tailgate.

A light drizzle was falling. I shut my eyes.

I heard the cab door twang, opened my eyes to see the light flowing from behind me, heard it slam shut. The light disappeared.

I felt Ed standing beside me.

"F-f-f-follow me."

"You want the light?"

"It's b-b-better without it."

He veered off the road to the right, onto a small path I hadn't seen. It led up a short way, then started down. The lapping sounded closer.

AT THE FAIR
1983

The year Alice was fourteen she did horses. She would not have been able to without the help of her uncle, Mort. He gave her the use of one of his, kept it in his field, bedded it in his barn, found the right saddle for it. Alice spent every afternoon after school over there, and all day on the weekends and during the summer.

Mavis encouraged this. "It makes up for the friends she doesn't have," she thought. Mavis worried about Alice. She had spent so much time by herself growing up. Even when people were available she always seemed to want to be alone.

Alice's interest in horses led her to enter the horse show at the fair outside Pierre the first weekend in September. Alice practiced ten hours a day preparing—jumps, canter, trot, slow walk.

In the weeks before the fair Alice was the most excited Mavis had ever seen her. She started dreaming out loud. "The top three riders win ribbons. What if I won one! A blue one, or a red one, or even a yellow one, hanging from Cozy's bridle. I might."

"Even if you don't, it's all right."

"You get to ride twice around the stadium while everyone cheers."

Later she said, "The top three in each class go to the state contest in Yankton. And the top three there go to the National Championships in Boulder, all expenses paid. Wouldn't that be something. And the winner there! I can't even think about it. A whole year traveling around doing shows!"

"You have to be pretty good to do that."

"Mort says I've gotten a lot better. And Cozy's great. The best horse he ever had. That's why he let me use her. If I win she's mine forever, he said. She might be anyway, for my birthday. He didn't say, but she might."

"That's nice, sweetie." Mavis smiled. "Just don't get your hopes up too much. Not everyone wins. Even people that are good."

Alice cut her short. "I know that."

The evening before the horse show Alice was so quiet Mavis kept looking at her to make sure she was all right. Several times she asked, "You okay?"

The first two times Alice nodded. The third time she erupted. "Yes, mom. I am fine! How many times do I have to tell you?"

"You know you don't have to do this if you don't want to."

"I want to." She spoke so quietly Mavis barely heard her.

"Mort's coming when tomorrow?"

"5:30."

"When should we get up? Four? Is that enough time? You'll need to do your hair."

"You don't need to come with me, mom."

Mavis caught her breath. "I can, if you want me to. I was planning on it."

Alice shook her head. "I think it'd be better if you didn't."

"Oh." Mavis was quiet. "Okay. If that's how you want it. Should I meet you in the place where the horses all gather—the, you know, what do they call it?" She smiled.

Alice studied her hands. "I'd rather you didn't."

Mavis looked at her, startled. "I won't be in the way."

Alice shook her head.

Mavis was quiet a long time. Alice stayed focused on her hands, took one quick glance at her mother, looked back down.

"You can do it any way that makes you feel better. It's your thing, as they say." Mavis started a laugh, but it died in her throat. "You know I'll be up there in the stands, cheering you on. What time does your group go on?"

"I don't want you to be there."

"You're my daughter, I . . ."

"If I go to Yankton you can. And Boulder. But not tomorrow, Mom. Please. It'll make me too nervous."

Mavis bit her lip, turned away. "What about the rest of the fair? Do I need your permission for that too?"

Alice came up behind Mavis, wrapped her long arms around her, hugged her tight. "Anything else you want."

Mavis stood stiff. She couldn't help noticing how much bigger and stronger Alice had become.

"I'm sorry, Mom. I'm not trying to be mean. Do you understand?"

There was a long silence. Alice's arms fell from her mother. No one spoke. Alice watched the back of Mavis's head. Neither one moved.

For Alice the silence was painful. As it went on, it hurt less. After a while it seemed arbitrary. Finally it seemed silly.

"I'm going to have some pie," she announced, as if everything was fine, a piece of the blueberry pie Mavis had baked for her that afternoon. "Would you like some?"

"I'm not hungry." Without looking back Mavis marched into her room, shut the door behind her.

Alice watched her go, her mouth half open, let out a long sigh, shrugged, and walked toward the kitchen.

Mavis didn't get up when Alice left. She heard Alice's alarm, heard the shower, her walking around, getting dressed, eating breakfast, Mort's truck pull up, their whispered voices, even, she thought, Alice's steps approach her door and stop. Still she stayed in her room with the door shut, pretending she was asleep.

She spent the morning preparing her preliminary income tax statement, four months before it was due, arrived at the fair in the early afternoon. She walked around, looking at the usual exhibits and displays, but she didn't see them. She was thinking of Alice, what she was doing, where she might be. "Now she's getting the horse ready," she thought, looking at her watch, "currying it, putting on the blanket and saddle."

"Now she's practicing her trots and her jumps," she said to herself, thinking how she was supposed to be there, watching and helping. Mavis's palms were cold. How nervous and excited Alice must be.

She pictured Alice in the new, western-style riding clothes she'd modeled the day before: her pointed brown cowgirl boots; faded jeans; light blue form-fitting shirt with the pearl snaps and white tassels; three inch silver earrings, dangling from each ear, her tan cowgirl hat, blond hair curling out from under it; and Mavis' last minute addition, a bright red bandana tied around her neck. How pretty she was. What an attractive young woman she'd become.

Mavis wanted so much for her to be happy. Anything to avoid this awful boredom and loneliness. But she didn't know what to do to help her. Maybe if she won.

Late in the afternoon, Mavis ended up at a food booth, got herself a hot dog and soda. Only when she sat on the grass eating did she realize how tired and hungry she was.

She looked up, saw riders on horseback passing, trotting briskly toward the horse show, walking slowly coming out. So many girls rode by, all done up in their finery, their hats pinned on, their lips bright red. She watched for Alice. All the girls were younger.

She looked to her left. She was right outside the ring. When the wind blew, she heard scattered half-phrases from the announcer.

She stood up, walked toward the entrance. She wanted to go inside, to sneak in and watch. And act afterwards as if she hadn't.

What if Alice saw her?

She wouldn't. There were hundreds of people in there.

Alice would. It'd be just her luck.

Mavis turned away, stopped to let more riders pass. It was as if a factory spewed out young girls on horseback.

She started walking in a circle around the outside of the ring.

Across from the ring people were going in to the arena that held the Ox Pull.

She hadn't been to the Ox Pull since Nate was alive. She remembered how much fun it'd been—sitting high in the bleachers, watching the men with their teams, the animals so strong and quiet. Nate had known most of the drivers, whispered to her about them while their teams pulled.

She walked in with the others, climbed to the next to the top row of the bleachers at the end closest to the horse show.

When she sat down she noticed how much cooler it had become. The sun had almost set; there was a nip to the air. She wished she'd brought warmer clothes. The breeze stirred. It was going to get cold that night.

She heard someone else. "Yup, won't be long before we're having snow."

"No!" she thought, "don't let it be winter yet. Please. Let the cold dark hold off a little longer." It was hard enough as it was. She didn't know how she'd manage until spring.

Below, to her right, lay the alley the girls rode on going to and from the horse show. They kept riding by, it seemed, without a break. She didn't know the county had so many girls. She kept watching, but didn't see Alice.

To the other side lay the rest of the fair. At the far end stood the ferris wheel, its smear of color turning up into the sky, dropping back down toward the earth.

The Ox Pull had just started. As she watched, she remembered how it worked. A stack of cement blocks stood in a pit. Each yoked pair had three chances to pull it seventy-two inches. After each team had its turn, more blocks were added, and the teams pulled again.

"Two oxen are paired from a young age," she heard the person behind her saying. "Even when they're only a couple of months old they have to practice wearing that wooden yoke. So they can learn to work together."

A little like marriage, she remembered thinking, when Nate had explained it to her.

She studied the teams, trying to decide which one to root for. She wanted Nate to be there, whispering in her ear, telling her who was who.

To her right, the riders trotting up toward the ring seemed older. In the distance she saw a red splotch around a girl's neck. She watched her approaching. It was Alice.

Mavis smiled, raised her hand to wave, held it frozen in the air. Tears formed in her eyes. Alice looked so pretty, in her new clothes, her hair sparkling, her lips bright red. "I love you," Mavis thought.

She wanted to point her out to the people around her. "That's my daughter. See her. With the red bandana. Isn't she lovely!"

Alice rode forward, hands gripping the reins, eyes straight ahead, bouncing in the saddle. Her face was tight. She looked grim.

"Oh, my poor baby," Mavis thought. "Relax. It doesn't matter if you don't win. There are other ways to get out of here." Though in six years she still hadn't thought of one.

As Alice trotted past her and into the ring Mavis touched her fingers to her lips. "Do well."

The bucket loader was adding a block to the weight. All the teams had gone once; none had been eliminated.

One of the team leaders was a woman. "Maybe I'll be for her," Mavis thought. She watched, decided not to. Something about the woman wasn't relaxed enough. She seemed afraid of the animals, as if she had no control over them.

Hers was the first pair eliminated. They didn't work as a team—one pulled left, the other right.

Another young leader no one liked. While his team pulled, straining under the weight, he yelled and cursed at them, cracked the whip on their backs, worked himself into a frenzy. When they'd pulled far enough, he almost crowed, strutting around like a rooster.

His was the second team eliminated. No one said anything, but she could tell everyone was pleased.

The others were harder to decide about. Six teams were left—different sizes, different colors—tan, black and white, brown. Their leaders were different sizes, shapes, ages; all seemed to know what they were doing.

Behind her Mavis heard a burst of applause. In the alley to the side a collection of girls rode by, leaving the ring. A few had ribbons attached to their horse's bridles. They trotted by. Others followed, clopping along.

At the third weight Mavis started to notice one of the teams and its leader. By the end of that round half of the teams had been eliminated. His was still in.

He was standing right below her, his back to her. There was nothing flashy about him. He was a youngish man, large, with big hands and arms, short hair under a feed cap, wearing red suspenders on dirty worn clothes that seemed half a size too small. He moved like one of the oxen—slow and steady, with a lumbering gait. He seemed calm, even gentle. He wasted nothing, exerted no extra energy.

With his team, he was remarkable. He never raised his voice, didn't even have a whip. He hardly talked to them.

Everyone else worked in pairs, one to lead, the other in back to guide the team and drop the chain over the weight. Not Red Suspenders; he worked by himself, just him and his team.

When his turn came, he walked behind the pair up to the pit, his rhythm the same as theirs. He backed them up to the weight, dropped the chain over the hook. They stood, waiting for his command. He walked to the front of the one on the left, laid his hand on its nose, said something to it, removed his hand. The team pulled forward, as one, hardly straining.

The crowd cheered, Red Suspenders unhitched them, walked them back to their spot, sat down in his folding lawn chair to wait his next turn.

Watching his team work Mavis felt a lump in her throat. They were good.

People around her liked them too. "Aren't they great?" "They won last year; remember?" "They're not big, either."

All the other teams were larger—one stood at least six inches higher—but no team pulled the weight as quickly or as easily.

The weight increased, and increased again, until only two teams were left—Red Suspenders and his matched jerseys and another, older man, with a pair of huge holsteins.

Another block was added. "7500 pounds," she heard someone say. "Almost four tons."

"This is it." The man beside her stretched.

The other team went first. On its three pulls, the farthest it got was forty-eight inches.

"Good job, Joe. Let's hear it for him, folks."

The crowd clapped.

"Joe mumble," it sounded like to Mavis. "From over Aberdeen. Always a good team, Joe. Beat your son this time too."

One of the other leaders, a younger man, waved.

It was Red Suspenders' turn. He had three pulls to beat forty-eight inches.

Mavis leaned forward to hear the announcer. She wanted to know who she was rooting for. He looked familiar. She wondered if he was someone Nate had known.

"Well, folks. This is it. Last turn. Three chances to beat that, Ed."

The crew pulled the weight back, raked the pit out.

"Folks, it couldn't end any better than this. Always a good team, fine, well-trained young animals, the winner here last year and at other contests all over the Upper Midwest. Ed Blanchard, from just up the road in Grasslands."

Chills ran down Mavis's back. She looked again. That was Ed! No wonder he looked familiar.

"Yeah, Ed!" she shouted to herself. "Come on. You can do it!"

That was the pair she had seen him training to the yoke when they were calves—behind the barn after chores, walking around and around, talking to them, stroking them, encouraging them, correcting them, never once raising his voice.

She smiled. They were good.

He and the team stood waiting until the raking was complete.

She glanced beside her. Girls rode away from the ring. She saw one—red bandana around her neck, blond hair curling out from under her hat. And no ribbons on the bridle. "Oh, Alice," she thought.

Her horse walked slowly. Her shoulders sagged. Mavis couldn't see her face. Just from her back she seemed defeated, but relieved too. Nothing about her was tense, her hands loosely holding the reins. "Oh, my poor girl," Mavis thought, "Oh, my baby."

She wanted to be there when Alice reached Mort's trailer, to take her, hold her, soothe the pain.

She stood up, sat back down. She'd see her later. When she got home. It'd be soon enough.

She'd come up to her with a smile, as if not knowing. "How'd it go," she'd ask, ready to say, "That's all right, I'm still proud of you," if that's what Alice needed.

She watched the red bandana disappear into the dusk.

To the side, white, yellow, green, red light turned up into the air over the dark plain, plunged back toward the ground.

On the grass in front of her Ed Blanchard lumbered with his

team up to the pit, backed them up to the weight, dropped the chain over the hook, and, as if he had all the time in the world, walked around to the front of the ox on the left, to talk to it quietly and put his hand on its nose.

Above the sky was dark purple; a few stars were already visible. The air had gotten colder. Goose bumps rose on her arms.

A BIG ONE
1985

Two weeks after Edna's marriage, Mort took Mavis and Ed walleye fishing. He asked Alice too, but she declined. She hadn't been out on a boat since Nate'd died.

They reached the boat slips just as the sun was setting. Mort backed the boat out, headed east into the twilight. The dark hills around them seemed to glow, as if the sky was their halo.

Ed and Mavis trolled while Mort drove, using different spoons and spinners.

Ed caught two walleyes, brought them into the net Mavis held out, beaming like a kid.

"Th-th-those'll m-m-m-make good eating, w-w-w-won't they?"

After a while Mort pulled in the throttle, killed the engine, let the boat drift in the breeze.

The sky had darkened to the color of the hills. Stars appeared, singly at first, then in clumps.

They each sat in chairs on the back of the boat, intent on their lines, the only sound the splash of a lure on the water, the click of a reel being turned in, the bluh-bluh of water under the boat.

Mavis caught a six-pound northern pike, was glad Ed jumped up to help land it.

"W-w-w-way to go," he said, smiling, as he put it on the stringer.

"Watch its teeth," Mort reminded from his chair.

"I k-k-know," Ed said, his large fingers held in the back corner of its mouth.

Mort hooked something, lost it reeling it in. One moment the line was taut, the next slack.

Ed landed another walleye. "Th-th-that makes th-th-three!" he shouted. "Th-th-they ain't much f-f-f-for f-f-fighting, but th-th-they're sh-sh-sure good eating." He grinned at Mort. "Y-y-you c-c-coming for dinner t-t-tomorrow, Mort?"

Mort smiled. "You catch any more, I'm bringing the family."

They hit a dry spell. No one caught anything for twenty minutes. Mort wondered about driving to another spot, decided not to. He didn't feel like moving. They'd drift into something after a while. Mort liked fishing, but he couldn't be bothered figuring out what spots were better than others, especially on water as large and varied as the reservoir.

The breeze picked up. Mavis put on her sweater.

Splash, click, retrieve, splash, click, retrieve.

Ed leaned his head back, stared straight up. The Milky Way ran across the middle of the sky.

"H-h-how m-m-many stars are there?" he seemed to ask the night.

"Bunches," Mavis answered.

"Mmm," said Mort.

"D-d-did you ever c-c-count them?"

Mort smiled, shook his head.

"I t-t-tried once."

"How many did you get?" Mort asked.

"I d-d-d-don't know. I l-l-lost track."

"Twenty?"

"M-more than th-that. A-a-almost a hundred."

Mort let his line drift, leaned back. "Did you ever wonder how many other solar systems might be out there?"

Mavis looked up. "A lot."

"You sound pretty sure."

"I have a lot of faith." She smiled. "Besides, I know there was no central focus to evolution. It happened all over the place simultaneously."

Mort pointed at the sky. "Even in space?"

She nodded. "It's one of the few things I'm sure about."

"So there might be creatures like us all over the place?"

"The sky's the limit."

Mort smiled, pointed his finger at her. "Not bad."

"Not only that, but all their rivers have walleyes and pike that they go fishing for. And some of them even have huge fish in them. 'Sturgeon in the sky' they're known as. To those who believe in them."

For a minute they both were quiet. Even Mavis had to admit it took a lot of faith to imagine earths and solar systems on pin points of light.

"Do you think we'll ever know about them?"

"Some day. I guess."

Mort looked across the thousands of stars visible in the Milky Way. "How will we find them?"

Mavis shrugged. "Luck." She kept looking up. Celestial people seemed to crowd the sky. She wanted to follow them home, find out more about them.

She looked over at Mort. "Do you think they're any happier than we are?"

Mort smiled at the breeze, the smell of warmth and water mixing in the night. "Nobody's happier than this."

"God help them."

A bright streak shot across the sky, hurtling toward the reservoir.

"Th-th-th . . ." Ed started to say, pointing.

"What, Ed?"

"A sh-sh-shooting star." It went dark before it reached the water.

The call of an owl echoed off the hills. Ed stiffened. It hooted a second time, fainter.

He smiled, sat up. "S-s-someone's g-g-gonna have g-g-g-good luck tonight." He turned his reel in, cast back out.

"Yeah," Mort said. "Guess who that is."

Splash, click, retrieve, cast, splash, click, retrieve.

A piece of the eastern horizon seemed to glow. A large moon emerged, got smaller as it climbed. One edge had a slice missing.

"T-t-two days after f-f-full," Ed said. "C-c-c-couldn't see it t-t-two nights ago. Overcast."

Mavis hooked something, started turning it in, lost it.

"You s-s-started turning in too f-f-fast. Y-y-you have to let it s-s-set the h-h-hook."

Mavis nodded.

"What do you say?" Mort asked. "Think we should move?

Ed's rod jerked out of his hand. He lunged forward, grabbed it.

"Falling asleep, Ed?" Mort asked.

Ed held on with both hands, tried to pull back. They felt the boat move backwards.

"Whoa," said Mort. "What was that?

"I've g-g-g-got s-s-something. A b-b-big one."

Line stripped off the reel.

"Wh-wh-what do I do?"

Mort stood beside him, staring at the water. "Let it take it."

After a few minutes the line went slack. Ed clicked the reel, started turning in. Every time he played the rod up it bent double. He lowered the tip before it snapped. He reeled in as quickly as he could, keeping the line tight.

"Wh-wh-what is it?"

A BIG ONE

"Something big. What line do you have on there?"
"Eight p-p-pound t-t-t-test."
"This ought to be fun."
Mavis stood at the edge, watching the water.
No matter how hard Ed turned the line stayed slack.
"You didn't lose him?"
Ed shook his head, turned faster.
"He's c-c-c-coming back t-t-toward us."
"He's not going to ram us, is he?"
For a minute Mavis had a vision of Nate in his smaller boat, as a gigantic who-knew-what crashed into it, sent him flying. She saw the same thing happening to them, all in slow motion, so that every moment was clear but there was nothing she could do to stop it. The hair on her arms stood on end. She gripped the side of the boat, waiting for the collision.
"Look!" Mort pointed toward the water thirty feet away. The largest fish any of them had ever seen leaped into the air. "What a monster!"
"It's a wh-wh-whale!" shouted Ed.
It landed with a splash and was gone. The line went taut, started stripping off the reel.
"Wh-wh-what do I do?" Ed lifted the rod. It bent double. He lowered the tip. The reel clicked as line pulled away. "N-n-nothing holds it."
"Let it run."
Ed released the reel. Line flew off it. They watched it go.
"Looks like he's headed for home."
"Wh-wh-where's that?"
"Main channel, I imagine."
"H-h-how far's that?"
"Six, eight miles east, two, three hundred feet down."
"I-I've only got h-h-half a mile of line."
"Guess we hope."
"N-n-n-nothing else to do?"

Mort shook his head.

They watched the water, dark but for sparkles of moonlight. Line pulled off the reel so fast it seemed to hum.

Ed smiled. "L-l-like a song." He hummed with it.

Mavis stared at the dark water, thinking of the monster of the deep, where he was headed, what buried sights he swam past. She was thrilled, now that he was moving away, and no longer afraid.

"N-n-not much l-l-line left."

"Try with the rod again, see if that'll hold him."

Ed clicked the reel. Line kept stripping off. He raised the rod. It didn't slow anything. He lowered the tip.

Mort shrugged. "Nothing you can do, I guess, with something that size."

They watched the last of the line whirl around. It reached the end and with a snap broke free.

For a moment Mavis saw the gleam of nylon monofilament snaking away on the surface. Then Ed's big one was gone, like a wild pet loose on a long leash, headed down toward its home among paintings of fish, buffalo, and a stick figure working while water lapped at his feet.

THE CATTLE BUYER
1987

I pulled in smooth and easy with all that power, came to a stop, slid the lever into park, and waited for the last of the line of dust to catch up with the car. I flicked on the wiper, watched it clean the thin film from the windshield, then shut the engine off. Even in the cool of the car my shirt stuck to my back. When I opened the door, waves of hot air washed in. I pushed myself out, stood up, stretched, moved my legs up and down, letting my clothes rearrange themselves, tucked my shirt back into my pants, redid my belt.

I stopped a moment, looked up and down the empty street, the almost deserted town, squinting from the heat and sun and dust, pulled open the wooden screen door, went inside the cafe. It was clean inside, and a little stuffy. There were six stools at the counter, two tables along the wall. I sat on one of the stools. No one else was in there. Women's voices came from in back; I'd heard them outside. I listened a minute, heard what sounded like "rosemary" and "remembrance," couldn't make out anything else they were saying. I picked up a menu, looked at it, looked around, waited. The voices went on. I cleared my throat. No one came.

"Hello?"

The voices stopped.

"Anybody there?"

"Be right with you."

It was a minute or two before one of them came out from in back and went behind the counter.

"Sorry. Didn't hear you come in."

I nodded. "It's all right."

She took a rag, wiped it across the clean counter, set out a glass of water. "What can I do for you?" She wiped the counter again.

"I don't know. I'm too late for dinner and too early for supper." I let out with a little laugh, but she just looked at me and didn't crack a smile. I let it die.

"I could make you up a sandwich." She looked at me again. "Depends on what you want."

I looked at my hands. "You still got any of that blueberry pie?"

"Special of the day."

"I'd try a piece of that."

"Coffee too?"

"With, thanks."

She set 'em in front of me. I ate slowly, glad to be in out of the glare. She wiped the counter from one end to the other, then stood looking at me.

"Good." The taste of crust and juice ran together in my mouth.

"Where you coming from?"

"Mobridge this morning. But Sioux Falls is home."

She nodded. "You ever been to California?"

"Couple times."

"You recognize a place like this?" She took a picture post card from the mirror behind her, laid it on the counter.

I glanced at it. "Looks like California."

"Is that what it looks like? With the flowers?"

"Some places." I slurped a little coffee.

"I have a daughter out there."

I looked at her. She didn't look old enough for a grown daughter, but I couldn't tell anymore.

"Bakersfield. You ever hear of it?"

"Mmm." I nodded.

She was studying the card. "What's it like there?"

"It's ok."

She didn't say anything.

"Depends on what you're looking for."

She put her finger down on one part. "Those flowers belong in that picture?"

I looked again. "How do you mean?"

"They didn't take a garden picture and paste it on?" Her finger followed the line.

"Yeah, maybe they did."

"That's what I thought. What's wrong, it's not pretty enough the way it is?"

I took another bite of the pie. "L.A. I was in. Fresno too. It's not all like that."

"I might go out and see her."

"Vegas is the place though. You ever been there?"

"I don't know if I might not be welcome."

She stood staring off behind me. I took a bite more, chewing slow. It was good, like grandma used to make. I wanted the taste to last.

She turned the card over on the counter. "There an address on there anywhere?"

I studied the writing. "Dear Mom," it started. I felt funny, reading other people's mail. I skimmed over it, trying not to read the message.

"Not that I see."

She nodded. "Didn't know if I might have missed it."

"It was sent from Bakersfield though." I tried to make out the date. "When'd you get this?"

"While back."

"That's what I thought." I took another bite of pie.
She wiped at the counter again.
"I don't know. Maybe she's not there anymore."
She settled in to staring at me, but it was like she didn't see me.
I finished the pie, wiped my mouth on the napkin.
"The berries fresh?"
"What's that?"
"The berries. Are they fresh?"
She nodded.
"Can't get fresh blueberry too many places."
"I've got my own bushes."
"They taste it."
"Reminds me of home."
"Where's that?"
"You want some more?"
"I don't need it."
"It's the special."
"Sure, why not."
She set another piece in front of me; filled my coffee too.
"I don't know if I can finish it."
"Eat all you want."
I picked the fork up, held it empty in the air, considering.
"You don't have any ice cream, do you?"
"Eight flavors."
"A little vanilla'd sure taste good with this. 'A la mode.'"
"Got blueberry too, if you want to try some."
"Blueberry ice cream?"
"Made it myself. Special of the day."
I couldn't decide. Vanilla was more what I had in mind.
"Yeah, ok. Let's give it a try."
She picked the plate up, took it away. When she brought it back there were two scoops of ice cream on top of the pie.
"How's that?"

I nodded. "Looks good."

I took a bite, chewing slowly. It was good, but I was just about full, my belly pushing against my belt.

She picked up the card, looked at it absently, put it back on the mirror. When she looked away I eased my belt out to the first notch.

She wiped the counter, poured out my water, gave me fresh, then just stood, arms crossed, not looking at anything. We were quiet a long time.

I ate slowly, savoring it. "Who's your friend?"

"Who's that?"

"That you've got out back."

She looked blank.

"You can tell her to quit hiding and come out here. I won't bite."

"No one's back there."

"I heard talking when I came in."

She got a funny expression.

I held the fork up, bits of ice cream and blueberry between the tines.

"That was me."

I nodded, licked the fork off, took another bite. I didn't think I could eat much more.

"Who was the other one?"

"You want to see who's back there?" She disappeared, came back with a flowered hat and a small mirror on a stand. She set the mirror on the counter, put on the hat, started talking in a different voice, watching herself in the mirror. Then she took the hat off and went back to her own voice, holding the hat in her hands.

"I, uh, act different parts."

I slurped a little coffee. "Any I might know?"

She shook her head.

"From TV?"

"We don't have much for reception out here."

"Say, you seen those dish antennas they have? All the motels've got 'em. You can pick up all over—Philadelphia, Saskatchewan, everywhere."

Her eyes widened. "They cost much?"

"Twenty-nine hundred, I think the man said. Which isn't bad, considering."

"Well, maybe not this week."

"They're all the rage."

She was quiet a minute.

"I do them from my head."

I gave a little burp. "Do one for me." I looked at the pie, the ice cream running over one edge, juice and berries oozing out from between the crusts, had another slurp of coffee.

"You already heard me."

"Do some more."

She had her hat in her hands, thinking.

"You're not a talent scout, are you?"

"Me?" I almost choked on the coffee. "That's a laugh."

"They have 'em in California."

"Maybe they do." I took a bite, and then another. Maybe I could stuff it all in.

"My daughter said. Los Angeles, anyway." She said it careful, like it wasn't a word she said much and she wasn't quite sure of the pronunciation.

She was still holding the hat.

"You gonna do one, or what?"

"You're the first customer today."

I took another bite. "Mmm?"

She nodded. "Except for Mort and Edna for coffee at ten." She stared off at the window.

I chewed slowly, the piece in my mouth mixing with the ice cream, cold at first, then melting.

"How long's the highway been open?"

"Must be five, six years now. Seems like forever."

I nodded. "Doesn't show on my map. Guess it's time for a new one." I swallowed. "I was by"—I took another bite—"must've been just before that. You couldn't hardly get in here."

She was quiet.

"I remembered the pie."

I put the last piece on my fork, studied it, wondering if maybe I shouldn't cut it in half, then popped the whole thing in my mouth.

"There's pancakes, too. Slump. All sorts of things."

"I saw the list."

I swallowed the last little piece, held my breath a second to make sure it was staying down.

"The milk shake's not bad."

I gave another little burp. "If I had one more bite, I think I'd bust."

"You could take some with you."

I shook my head. "Thanks." And came out with a full-sized belch that echoed off the walls, settled things around inside. " 'Scuse me."

"Not even another piece of pie?"

I wiped my mouth. "Maybe some pie."

"For later?"

"Sure."

She cut a big piece, wrapped it, laid it on the counter in front of me. Wasn't much left to the one I'd started.

I mostly finished the coffee and pushed the cup back, but I didn't get up. It was quiet; quiet and hot. Behind the counter a fly buzzed. She frowned, turned and watched it.

I sat a while, pushed the stool back a little.

"You don't have to go?"

"Got to get to Faith tonight, and I got a stop to go."

"Now?"

"Auction's first thing in the morning, and I still got to look over the stock."

"You a buyer?"

I nodded.

"Oh."

I looked at my hands.

"A lot going out, hunh?"

"A guy's got to make a living."

I let out with a little fart. She didn't seem to notice.

"Buy low?"

"People have to eat."

She looked at me a long time, then picked the hat up off the counter, turned it around in her hands, put it on, looked at herself in the mirror, took it off, turned to me.

"Buy the cafe, mister."

I looked at her. "It's cattle I buy."

"I'd let you have it cheap."

I turned the ring around on my little finger.

"Think it over. And when you come back through . . ."

I felt for my itinerary. It was with my jacket in the car.

"I don't know when that might be."

"It's got a good location, regular clientele, must be a year's supply of blueberries in the freezer."

"I've got to be in Williston the day after tomorrow. Miles City the day after that."

"Taking advantage of everybody?"

"I don't make them sell. All I do is buy."

I pushed back the stool and stood up.

"You don't set the prices too?"

I looked at her.

"There's some that do. Get together with the other buyers and agree not to bid."

"Well, I'm not one of those. I work by myself."

I was quiet a minute, twisting the ring around and around.

"In Mobridge this morning I was high bidder on a lot. Afterwards they were all yelling at me, and nasty, like it was my fault. What am I supposed to do, bid against myself?" I looked down at the empty plate, the remains of the pie I'd come for. "And the shippers complain if I pay too much." I took the fork, pushed around a few crumbs and some juice I'd missed. "It's a helluva way to make a living."

"I know what you mean."

There was another pause.

"I remember when my folks went out. During the depression."

She just nodded.

The two of us stayed quiet a long time, like there was so much more to say, but we didn't neither one know what it was or how to say it.

"Say, it can't be too far to the Blanchard place, can it?"

She stiffened. "Ed?"

"Think that's it. I might as well stop there while I'm here."

"You're like a vulture."

"I don't call myself up and tell me to come."

"Hasn't he had enough trouble already?"

"If it's not me it'll be someone else."

We were quiet a minute.

"It's just down the road on the right. That it?"

She didn't answer.

"I can ask across the road if you'd rather."

She turned toward the front of the cafe, stared out the window. "You can't miss it."

I nodded. "Well."

She turned back. "There isn't anything else I can get you?"

I shook my head. "Pie was real good though. And the ice cream too." I picked up the wrapped piece.

"Wait." She busied around for a minute. "Ice cream won't keep in this heat, but what about something like this?" She handed me a large container, with a cap and a straw. Inside was a blueberry milk shake.

"Thanks. I appreciate it."

I set them down, peeled her off a ten. Her eyes were on the rest of my roll.

"That do it?"

She nodded, moved toward the cash register.

"Keep it."

Her mouth formed part of a smile. "Thanks."

I picked the pie and shake back up, started for the door.

"Think it over, won't you?"

I pushed open the screen, stepped outside.

Her voice followed me out. "I'm willing to come down."

The screen swung shut behind me.

I stopped two steps out the door, adjusting to the light and heat and dust. The whole car needed wiping off, light brown dirt visible all over the maroon; just polished too.

I looked up at the sun. Still a couple more hours before it started getting cooler.

When I got to the car I heard her voices again. I stopped by the door a minute and listened, thinking about sliding onto the seat, maybe undoing my belt and the top button of my pants, and sipping at the milk shake while I drove.

ED BLANCHARD
1986

Ed had good ideas about running a farm. He knew how many steers the land would support, how to mix hay and pasture fields to get the most out of both, where to graze the sheep to get the best yield from them. When the price fell on calves, he drove all over eastern South Dakota and western Minnesota, going from dairy farm to dairy farm, buying day-old calves. He raised them as veal on milk replacer and made a good profit.

Ed and Edna had inherited the farm after their father died. She took care of the business and bookkeeping, he did all the farm work. He knew every domestic animal on the place. He could tell how each one was feeling by looking at it, by how it stood, by the way it baaed or mooed. He remembered where he'd gotten each one, for how much, how old it was, how well it ate, how quickly it grew, how big it would get, how much it'd bring.

When Ed brought his calves home, he hand-fed each one for a week, scratching its ears, talking to it, while it slurped on the bottle. When they were larger, grazing on the range with the others, they never forgot him. When he walked into a pen of thousand-pound steers, they nuzzled him with their wet noses, licked the salt on his arm with their rough tongues, while he rubbed behind their ears and called them each by name.

Edna went with him when he took the steers to market, to handle the financial transactions and make sure no one took advantage of him. They spent hours together in the cab of the cattle truck, bouncing over back roads. From time to time Ed whistled. He didn't know many songs. His favorite was "Yankee Doodle." Sometimes he repeated it over and over for fifty miles. And, for long stretches, they were quiet.

The buyers and auctioneers treated Ed fairly. They respected him for the steers he produced, gave him a good price. Edna no longer went along out of necessity, but for companionship, out of habit. The few times she didn't go, Ed said he didn't mind, but he allowed as how he didn't whistle as much.

When she wasn't around, he wasn't the same. He did all the work himself—she rarely came to the barn—but her presence, the idea that she was near, calmed him. When she was gone, he did a chore, proceeded with other chores, stopped, unsure if he'd done the first one, and remained befuddled, paralyzed by doubt. Eager to do well, he did the chore a second time, but for hours afterwards he felt unsettled, as if what he'd done wasn't right.

One June Ed stayed by himself for a week while Edna visited their cousin Alma in Centralia, Illinois. When she came back, she hummed all the time, danced by herself, smiling, and said, "Changes are coming, Ed. Big changes."

Ed nodded and smiled back. "Changes."

There'd been changes, too, while she was gone. Confused, Ed thought he'd missed a feeding of his calves, fed them an extra time. They got the runs from the excess. He panicked, fed them a third time, then a fourth. The worse their diarrhea got, the more he fed them; the more he fed them, the worse it got. By the time Edna came back, one calf had died. One died a day later. The others were sick for a week.

For the Fourth of July Edna brought her intended home. She

wanted Ed to like Steve, but Ed was bothered by changes. He wanted to go on running the farm with Edna the way they always had. All this activity, excitement and upheaval made him dizzy.

Six weeks later Edna married Steve at Aunt and Uncle Thayer's in Highmore. Ed gave her away.

"You look dazzling," she kept telling him, admiring his white jacket and the flower in his lapel.

The jacket seemed to have shrunk since he tried it on. Every time he moved it bound him under the arms.

He kept forgetting the flower was there. Several times during the ceremony he looked around, puzzled, trying to figure out where the sweet smell was coming from.

Afterwards Edna took him by the hand. "Come, I want you to meet all the pretty girls."

Each one they approached, he drew back, tugging on his sleeves. "Wh-wh-wh-what do I say? T-t-t-tell me what to say."

She laughed. "Say whatever you feel like. Just be yourself."

Twice he blurted out, "V-v-v-veal was ninety-seven cents last week," and "If we d-d-d-don't get some rain, all the sh-sh-sh-shit in Texas won't make nothing grow," a phrase he'd heard the week before at the auction. The people he said that to acted surprised or offended. After that the best he did was smile and nod, tug on his sleeves, and lift first one foot and then the other. No matter how long Edna kept someone in conversation, she still walked away before Ed was able to say anything.

Uncle Tower didn't help. A dozen times he came up to Ed, asked in a loud voice, "So, Ed, and when are you getting hitched?" and broke into peals of laughter. Ed's large face got hot all over, his jacket grew even tighter.

Edna started the first dance with him. A long line of men cut in. Ed drifted to the side, watched Edna dance away. From time to time he caught glimpses of her, his face lighting up at the sight. Before long he'd lost track of her. By the time she came looking for him he was gone. He left behind his rented jacket with the flower in the lapel, draped across the front seat of Steve's car.

The happiest he was all day was when he was back home doing the evening chores and milking the jersey cow he had hand raised from a calf. Harmony, her name was. It was a word Edna'd used. He liked the sound of it. "Harmony," he used to say, even before he had the calf. "Harmony. H-H-H-Harmony. Harmony."

While he milked her he described the wedding to her. "All the food and p-p-p-people and cars, Harmony; and so many p-p-p-pretty girls." He patted her brown flank. "And the colors, the different c-c-c-colored dresses. You just want to look at them, and touch them in your f-f-f-fingers. And the n-n-n-noise. Everyone talking, and p-p-p-people dancing, and a man with a d-d-d-drum. That'd startle your ears, I can tell you." He scratched her ears, stood up with a pailful of milk, ready to lead her out.

Steve Hagen sold computers for a firm out of Sioux Falls. He and Edna lived in the family house with Ed. Steve commuted twice a week, stayed over at his mother's two nights; the other nights he was home with them. Edna was always there, but things were different. Changes. Edna talked to Steve so much on the phone when he wasn't there. And when he was, they spent long periods by themselves in the room that used to be Ed and Edna's parents, with the door shut, talking and laughing.

If they were quiet too long, Ed knocked on the door. "Edna?"
"Yes?"
"It's m-m-me."
"What, Ed?"
"What are you d-d-doing?"
"It's all right, Ed. We're resting. We'll be out in a bit."

Edna never went with him in the cattle truck anymore. Ed said he didn't mind, but he didn't do much whistling.

Steve and Edna built a new house for themselves on the far corner of the property, three miles by road. It was an energy efficient unit they designed themselves, with in-ground construction, passive solar heat, and wind-powered electricity. They moved in for their first anniversary, but couldn't get Ed to leave the old house.

For days Edna didn't see Ed. She did talk to him on the phone, but Ed didn't like phones. He didn't say much. He didn't understand how the voice flattened into a box was Edna's.

In answer to her questions he nodded or shook his head. Sometimes all he said was "Edna. Edna?"

More and more often Ed got confused, was on the verge of making major errors, when Edna stopped by, and by her presence made things right.

"You didn't feed them already," she asked, as he started to feed the calves.

He stopped. "I d-d-d-don't know."

"What did you just do?"

"I m-m-milked Harmony."

"What did you do before that?"

"I d-d-don't remember."

"What do you usually do?"

"I c-c-c-come out here, from the house." He stopped.

"Don't you usually feed them first.

"Yes."

"And what's this?" She held up the bucket with fresh lumps of milk replacer around the edge.

"I f-f-f-fed them!"

The lot across from the house was for sale. Ed wanted to buy it.

"It's a lot to spend."

"It'll s-s-save me money. I can grow c-c-corn there. That's f-f-f-feed I don't have to buy for the s-s-steers in the winter."

"And for that you need a harvester, and how much are they going for?"

"And my c-c-costs go down. I can put the c-c-cottonwood field in corn. And when the p-p-p-price of corn goes up, I don't c-c-care."

"You really think so?"

He nodded.

"I suppose."

More changes happened Ed didn't understand. Big changes. Interest rates started climbing. In six months payments on the new land and equipment doubled. Farmers sold their cattle to offset the rise in expenses. The price of cattle fell. The farm's income stopped paying its expenses. For a while Edna made up the difference out of savings. Interest rates rose again. The price for cows fell further.

Edna started going to auctions with Ed. They trucked as far as Sioux Falls, Ed whistling "Yankee Doodle," Edna grim and worried, staring out at the countryside that seemed dotted with abandoned farms. The price was so low she made him bring the animals back.

"Why wouldn't they b-b-b-buy them, Edna? Why wouldn't they give a b-b-b-better price?"

She shrugged.

"They're g-g-g-good animals. No one raises b-b-b-better. You can see that l-l-l-looking at them. C-c-c-can't you?"

It was a long, quiet ride home.

At Mobridge, the next week, the price was ten cents a pound lower. Afraid of what the following week would bring, Edna sold them.

Ed was happy going back. "They l-l-l-liked them better there. I t-t-told you!" He whistled most of the way.

Edna didn't see how they could keep paying for the new land.

"Why? It's g-g-g-good land. It k-k-k-keeps costs down."

The week before Ed was going to harvest the corn, a farmer

came from out of state and took the harvester. There was an altercation of some sort while the man was there, Edna found out later. Ed'd had to be restrained while the harvester was being loaded onto the truck. Ed'd called her when the man drove in, couldn't reach her. By the time she learned about it, the man and the harvester were gone.

Ed wanted to ask her, Why? What'd he done wrong? But for days she didn't come.

One time she tried. She drove down the road toward the house. Just before the dip, where it disappeared from view, she saw him sitting on the porch, staring at the field across the road. He looked so small and sad, as if he'd never understand or forgive what she'd done. She drove past without stopping.

One week went by, then a second, a third. Still she didn't call or visit. A few times Ed came into the house to hear the phone ringing. By the time he reached it the line was empty.

Day after day he sat on the porch, watching the corn mature, go past its prime, rot, saw it blown over by a wind storm, beaten down by rain, picked over by crows, ruined by a freeze.

He stopped leaving the property. For days he saw no one. He sat on the porch, staring at the field of decaying corn until it was too dark to see. Still he sat, waiting for a familiar pair of headlights to drive down the road.

A coyote got into the sheep field. It killed a market-weight lamb. He found it the next morning. Two days later there was another sheep dead, a prize ewe, pregnant out of season. Exposed where her flank was ripped open were triplet lambs, ready to be born. He stroked her head, talking to her: "Cynthia. Cy-Cy-Cynthia. Cynthia." He pulled the floppy lambs out, still in their sacs, and cuddled them, the salty fluid oozing over his hands, sticking to his fingers.

That night he sat up all night in the field, watching, the shotgun on his knees. He started to doze off. He was startled awake by the bleat of a lamb. He stood up, gun raised, ready to shoot at an imagined noise. He saw, grey in the moonlight, the field of grazing sheep. That changed to the perfect stalks of corn shrivelling before his eyes. He pitched forward, caught himself, stood swaying. The field was clear. His eyes started shutting. He shook his head, slapped his face, forced them open. He looked around, saw the sacs of the triplets, lion-sized.

A loud noise woke him. He jumped up from the ground, grabbed the gun lying beside him, ready, alert. His ears rang. Thirty feet away a lamb bleated, walking round and around in small circles, dragging its bleeding hind legs.

Ed ran to the wounded animal, loaded the gun, put the point of the barrel behind its ear, pulled the trigger. He sat on the ground, cradling the dead lamb in his arms, rocking back and forth, his pants staining with the warm liquid that quickly cooled and chilled him.

When he opened his eyes it was dawn. He was still holding the lamb. His arms were stiff, blood caked on his pants. He laid the lamb on the ground, dusted it with a handful of soil. He made the sign of a cross. "Rest in p-p-peace, little lamb."

The sun rose. Another clear, silent day. Ed, chilled, stood, looked over the field. All was calm. He walked back toward the barn, his pants clanking against his leg.

From the second field he heard a cow bellowing. He couldn't remember the last time he'd milked Harmony.

He found her standing in the stock pond, her bag packed hard. "Maaah! Maaaahhh!!"

He waded in, tried to lead her out. Each time they reached shallow water she drew back.

"Does the w-w-water feel good on your bag?" He stood in water up to his thighs, stroked her head, rubbed her ears. "You w-w-wait. Ed'll make it b-b-better."

He brought back a stool. He sat in water half way up his chest, started milking her. Jets of white squirted into the brown water, leaving light streaks that darkened as they spread.

She kicked at him as he milked.

"Easy, g-g-girl. It's all right, H-H-Harmony. I know it h-h-hurts."

Ed jerked to avoid a kick, slipped off the stool. He slid backward, sat on the murky bottom, his knees over the stool, his hair floating on the surface. He braced his hand on the muck beside him. Before he could stand, Harmony stepped on his foot.

Ed couldn't move. He waved his hands in the air. He flailed his arms in the water.

She stood pressing down on his foot.

He opened his eyes. Strange brown light was all around. He tried to lift himself. He couldn't.

He tried to talk to her. Water filled his mouth. He started coughing. More water flowed in. He swallowed some, coughed, swallowed more.

He kicked at her with his other foot. His lungs felt about to burst.

In her slow way Harmony lifted her leg.

Ed got his foot free, lunged up. His head shot out of the water. He gasped, drawing fresh air in. He kept rising, leaning against her, coughing and gasping, spitting out water.

"It's okay, H-H-H-Harmony," he got out between breaths, "it's m-m-me. Come on, g-g-girl. D-d-don't you remember Ed?"

She turned, started walking back into deeper water. He couldn't stop her. He followed, talking, consoling.

She stopped with the water half-way up her haunches. He started milking again. Bent over, the water at his nostrils, he reached under her, squeezed. He milked until the water around her was white.

She wouldn't let him lead her out. She stood, still mooing, in water four feet deep. Ed waded away from her, out of the pond.

He called the number for the vet, his clothes making puddles on the floor. He got a recording. The office was moved to Pierre. It gave another number. Twice more he called, trying to remember the new number. He repeated it to himself. He thought he had it. He started dialing. He got confused. The phone made strange noises.

He called Edna's number. No answer. He tried again. Old Mrs. Lundquist answered. What was she doing at Edna's? Why wouldn't she put Edna on? Where was Edna? She hadn't moved?

It took him five tries to get information. He couldn't remember her new name. They gave him his number.

He sat, receiver in his hand, listening to the "bnnhhgh, bnnhhgh" of the busy signal. "Edna. Edna?"

He put the receiver back on the hook. The noise stopped. He sat watching the phone, waiting for it to ring.

He heard the sound of distant bleating. He grabbed the gun, ran out. The sky was blue, the air calm. Everything was fine.

He spent the rest of the day in the sheep field. He heard Harmony bellowing. He started to leave. Before he reached the edge of the field the sheep started running. He turned back.

He spent the night in the field.

Bleat—moo—baa—maah he heard. The sounds mixed together. Moo—bleat—maah—baa. Maah—baa—maah—baa—moo—bleat. He couldn't find where they were coming from. Moo—baa—bleat—maah echoed as if hidden in caves. Maybe he only imagined them.

In the morning he found Harmony, floating in the middle of the pond, her large cow eyes staring up at nothing. Ed tried to reach her, bring her to shore. The water was too deep.

He sat on his stool at the edge of the pond, staring out at her. For a long time he stayed in the stillness, the only sound his dead cow bellowing within him.

He noticed three vultures, specks at first, coming closer. Lower and lower they circled until they almost touched her back.

Ed yelled. He waved his arms. Down they came. He loaded the gun with bird shot. One landed. Boom. He fired. They flapped their wings, flew up. He reloaded, fired again. One dropped into the water beside the cow. The other two kept rising.

All morning the two black birds circled above the pond, gliding around and around.

In the middle of the afternoon the drone of a small plane broke the silence. The sound startled Ed. He jumped up, searched the sky for it. He located it, high in the east. He stood, head craned up, as it approached. It flew over him, turned, flew over again.

Again and again it flew over, dipping, swinging, gliding, going around and around. Its noise was like a fly, buzzing deeper and deeper into Ed's head, vibrating off his skull louder and louder. He couldn't stand it anymore.

"G-g-go away!" he yelled, waving his arms.

The plane flew around again.

"Leave m-m-me alone!"

A vulture landed on Harmony's back, pecked at the flesh along her spine. Ed yelled, waved his arms. The vulture didn't move.

The other one landed. Two black spots pecked on her brown back. With each peck sections of hide disappeared.

Ed fumbled in his pocket for bird shot.

The buzzing returned.

He loaded the gun, took aim, fired into the air.

The plane flew on, turned, started back toward him.

The vultures kept pecking.

He hurried to reload.

OLD BONES

1988

The morning after Marvin Pembroke died, Mavis took the pointed shovel from the back hall, walked up the road toward the cemetery with it over her shoulder. She moved slowly, thinking about Marvin and his life, wondering how Mort would take his death.

There was a nip in the air, the hint of colder weather to come. She wore Nate's old carny windbreaker, several sizes too large for her, frayed at the collar and cuffs. She stopped, zipped it up, proceeded on.

Before she reached the cemetery she saw Mort's truck, parked in front. She expected to find him working. He was sitting on an upside-down bucket beside his mother's grave, leaning forward, his forearms above his knees, staring at her stone. His tools lay in the grass beside him.

He looked up when Mavis came in the gate, smiled at her.

She walked up to him, took his hand, squeezed it. "How are you doing?"

He nodded.

"I'm sorry."

He shrugged. "It's not a surprise."

The sadness in his voice surprised her.

"The remarkable thing is how long he hung on. He could hardly breathe. These last few days. 'Old Bones', he used to call himself. He'd say, 'Old Bones'—wheeze—'isn't going to'—wheeze—'be around'—wheeze—'much longer.' "

Mavis nodded, put her hand on Mort's shoulder. He reached up, rested his hand on hers.

She read the letters on his mother's stone, remembered digging the hole. It seemed so long ago.

She looked down at Mort, squeezed his shoulder, let her hand fall to her side.

"You looked sad," she said, "sitting here."

He nodded. "No matter how much you expect it, you don't feel it until it happens."

Mavis looked around.

Her sudden movement startled Mort. "What?"

"Where's his grave?"

"Whose?"

"Your father's."

"I haven't started it."

"He didn't dig it himself?"

Mort stared at her. His brows contracted. "No."

"He used to say he would." Mavis was quiet, thinking about Marvin. "Maybe he didn't get around to it."

Mort nodded. "Guess he figured I'd do it for him."

"I'll help."

"Thanks."

They both stood, staring ahead. Mavis wondered what Mort was thinking about.

She stuck her hands in her jacket pockets. "Where should we put it?" She took a few steps to the side. "Next to hers?"

Mort shrugged.

"That's what I'd think."

" 'In the corner,' he kept saying these last few days. 'Put me in the corner.' "

Mavis pointed toward the back. "With the tomahawks and arrowheads?"

Mort nodded.

Mavis thought about it. She'd never gotten around to digging back there.

Mort looked from where they sat to the corner, back to where they sat.

"We could move her stone," Mavis suggested.

Mort smiled, held up a finger. The gesture reminded her of Nate.

Mort stood up, picked up his tools. "Should we?" He started toward the back.

Mavis walked beside him with her shovel. He stopped in the corner. Mavis scuffed at the dirt. She didn't see any arrowheads.

Mort looked around. "I suppose one spot's as good as any other." He paced off six feet. "How's this?"

Mavis nodded. "Looks all right." She walked with her shovel to one corner, placed the point on the ground.

Mort stopped her. "Let me. I wanted to start with this."

He laid his shovel down, picked up his other tool. Mavis noticed it for the first time. It was the stone hoe from his desk.

He stood with it raised. "I wanted to return him to the land as best I could." He looked around. "I don't know exactly how to do it, but this seemed appropriate."

With the hoe he marked out the boundary of the hole, then broke the surface up throughout the inside. He worked slowly, carefully, as if, Mavis thought, out of reverence for the tool and the ceremony he was participating in.

When he'd scoured the entire surface he examined what he'd done. "Now we can dig." He laid the hoe down, picked up the shovel.

He started digging at one end, Mavis at the other. The soil was sandy and full of rocks. She tossed them to the side, kept digging.

The sky brightened, then darkened more. The mackerel sky furrowed its brow, she thought. The wind seemed colder. Digging warmed her body but chilled her hands. She stopped, moved her fingers back and forth, blew on them, turned her back to the wind.

Mort worked more slowly. He threw one shovelful out, stopped, put the shovel down, sifted through the sand with his fingers, held up some small rocks. "These are arrowheads. That we're throwing away."

Mavis turned to look.

"I'll bet you have some too."

Mavis set the shovel aside, kneeled down, picked up a stone from the pile, examined it. She was about to toss it away.

Mort stopped her. "That's one there. See the chisel marks on the side?"

She looked more closely. "I was expecting something, I don't know . . ."

"More clearly defined?"

She smiled, pointed her finger at him.

"This isn't exactly 'high art'," he said. "It's Indian functional. Whatever works."

"I thought they were just rocks."

She picked up three more. They all had marks on them. So did others around them. "They're all over."

Mort nodded.

"What was this? a meeting ground?"

"They probably made them here, or traded them."

She studied one. "How old are they?"

"A hundred, two hundred years. The farther down we get the older they are."

"Are they worth anything?"

"Not much. Maybe down farther."

Mavis rubbed her hands together, blew on them, started digging again. "I should have worn gloves."

From time to time she stopped, put her hands in her pocket. Anything to get them out of the wind.

She piled likely looking stones together, to sort through later. If she didn't stop she was almost warm enough.

Mort worked behind her. He stopped more often, tossed more rocks aside.

For long periods they didn't talk, the only sound their shovels scraping stone and sand, and the steady noise of the wind.

It went slowly, even with two.

They dug beneath their ankles. A mound rose between them. They turned, faced each other, lowered the raised section. Twice their shovels clanged together. They smiled, kept working.

"You heard from Alice recently?" Mort tossed a shovelful of sand out.

"No." Mavis kept digging. "Why?"

"I had a card from her."

"Oh?"

"A while back."

Mavis stopped, her foot on the top of the shovel. "Where from?"

"California, I think it was."

"How's she doing?"

"Ok."

Mavis stood still. Wind rushed past her. "Any word about coming back?"

"Didn't mention it. Just a friendly sort of how are things here. And she asked about Cozy."

What about me? Mavis wondered, did she mention me? knowing by the way he said it she hadn't.

"Remind me to let you take a look at it."

Mavis nodded. The sky seemed a uniform grayness, as if the weather would just skip through the rest of October and November right into winter.

She wished he hadn't told her about the card.

She watched the wind blow some light back into the clouds, pushed down on the shovel with all her weight.

A familiar sound made her stop.

"Geese," Mort said.

Mavis looked up, squinted, searching.

Beside her Mort's hand and finger pointed higher than she'd been looking. Dots of black formed a V against the sky. Honk—honk honk—honk—honk—honk. Their calls made the hair rise on her arms.

One group in a line broke away from the others, seemed to float into the middle of the V. The lines shifted. The V re-formed.

"Sixty-five," Mort said. His neck was back.

Mavis smiled. "Nice," she thought.

"A hundred years ago"—he talked toward the clouds—"the sky was black from morning til night."

"With geese?"

He nodded.

She tried to imagine the air filled with birds. Their honking must have been deafening.

She looked back up. The V was barely visible, its pattern shifting again.

One last honk floated down. It echoed around her as if coming from a cave that went farther and farther back in time until it reached a place before people were there.

Did the ancestors of these geese fly over then, she wondered, even if no one heard or saw them?

The sky was empty.

Mavis turned, pushed the shovel back into the dirt.

Beside her Mort still rested. "Carol didn't want me doing this." He picked at the shovel handle. "Didn't want to know anything about it. Didn't want the kids seeing it either. Said it was too primitive."

Mavis felt cold. She listened while she dug.

"I've got him in the back of the pick up. Under the tarp."

Mavis nodded. She'd noticed the lumpy canvas.

"No coffin. No cremation. Just his body. Naked as he came into the world."

Mavis thought about the two of them carrying him back there, wrapped in canvas, lowering him into the ground, wondered how difficult that would be.

"Carol went off about that too: 'Anybody sees you, you'll get arrested, carrying your father's naked body around in the back of your truck.'" Mort shrugged. "Maybe this doesn't fit anyone's religion. But it seems the thing to do."

Mavis didn't say anything. She nodded and kept working. She hoped Mort saw her.

"Nothing between him and the elements."

That time she caught his eye before she nodded.

They kept digging. Another mound rose between them. Their shovels clanked three times removing it.

The arrowheads were fewer but simpler. Their points were sharper.

"More clearly defined," he pointed out.

It wasn't so cold, working down out of the wind. Mavis' hands warmed up. She unzipped her jacket half way.

They were down to their waists. A.D. 1150 Mort guessed, and still going down.

Mort stopped digging, pried and pulled, raised a bone, in a moment brought up another one, held them above his head. "Look what I've got here. It's part of a skeleton."

Mavis looked over. "Indian?"

He nodded. "Probably. It wasn't very big, whatever it was." He shook the dirt off them. "There are people who can look at it—the shape of the bones, the size of the skeleton—and tell you how old he was, whether he had smallpox or died in battle—but I'm not one of them."

Mavis peered over his shoulder as he scraped dirt away. She

thought she could make out part of its shape—a foot, a calf bone, pelvis, chest, an arm. What Mort held were thigh bones.

He tapped them together over his head. They sounded hollow. He hit them together again, a little harder. He banged them together.

"Music." He smiled. "Dead man's waltz." He beat out different rhythms. "When we lay him in the ground we can dance around outside, give him a rousing send off."

Chills ran down Mavis' spine. She wanted him to stop. What he was doing might call spirits from all the bodies buried there, send them out on the wind scurrying over the plain.

She clutched her shovel with one hand, looked around, alert, as if the noise she heard wasn't the wind but spirits hurrying along. She felt them all around her.

In another minute Mort stopped. The wind turned back to air.

Mort tossed the two bones up onto the ground. They clacked together landing.

For a moment everything was still, as if even the wind had been chased away. The spirits settling back in their places, Mavis thought.

Mort picked up other bones, three or four at a time, set them down with a clatter, jumbled together.

"No wonder he's dead," Mavis pointed. "No head."

Mort nodded. "I doubt we'll find it. The Indians made circles of skulls. To keep the bad spirits away."

Mavis wondered if that was her problem, that she stood in the middle of her own circle of skulls, surrounded by all the people she'd lost. The vision frightened her—one of the eyeless heads she imagined grinning at her was Nate, one her father, one her mother, another Gladys, even Marvin. And one her own.

Above, gray clouds skittered across the sky, running from winter.

She had to get out of Grasslands before she ended up buried there herself.

She couldn't see herself laid out among the other bones and stones scattered around the bare yard. It sounded worse than living there.

She stood with a foot on the shovel and thought about leaving. She wondered how she might do it.

Maybe when the fair came around again in September. Nate had, when he was her age. Alice had too. Why not her? There didn't seem to be any other way.

She tried to picture walking into the carny, asking if they needed help. She didn't know. She couldn't see herself standing at one of the booths, pretending to smile, when everything inside hurt.

A gust of wind blowing over the hill brought her back to the graveyard. It whirled between gravestones, swirled the dust, moved on.

If the wind could do it, why couldn't she?

It wouldn't hurt to try.

Behind her Mort tossed one last bone up. She turned back to her work.

MIDSUMMER'S NIGHT
1989

Night was the time of terror for Mavis.

Days she could manage. The light was reassuring. Nothing was left to imagination. Each night was a battle. Nights were worst in winter, but even at their briefest they were full of danger.

June twenty-first was like the day before it and the day before that. Each one was perfect—warm, clear, dry. As a group their perfection was crushing.

Mavis kept the cafe open until six. The last customer had left at two-fifteen. Keeping it open meant not turning around the sign in the door that said "We're Open, Come On In" on one side, "Sorry, We're Closed, Please Call Again" on the other.

There were twelve hours to fill before Mavis turned the sign around, announced to the empty street that the cafe was open. As soon as she closed she began the strategies designed to get her to the dawn.

She didn't eat yet. She postponed supper as long as possible. She went out into the dusty heat of the late afternoon and walked along the glaring road past the abandoned post office and grocery store, the empty hardware and pharmacy and other boarded up, false-fronted buildings. They had been unoccupied so long no indication remained of what they once had been, the lettering on their signs faded and illegible.

At the end of town sat the small white church, beside it the cemetery. Without glancing at it she turned around. The church still looked clean and kept up. Since Reverend Almquist's retirement it was rarely used. She walked down the other side of the road, past other closed stores—Hilda's notions, Olson's Feeds and Seeds, Myrdahl's Farm Equipment, a tree. England's Auto, New and Used, Bought and Sold, was next, a white, windowless, flat-roofed building with a paved car lot beside it. Grass grew through the cracks of the lot, circled the sign on the post that was out of date when she'd moved there: Studebaker.

Across from the cafe, and her apartment above it, sat a vacant lot, waist high in weeds, grass, daisies and black-eyed Susans. Beyond it, rolling grasslands surrounded the town for miles in every direction. In a few years, she was sure, the sun, the wind, the dust and the rain would destroy all the buildings. Even the church, unused, unrepaired, would sag and fall in on itself. All a person driving through would know of what had been there would be the road he drove on. Waving grasses would crowd against the edge, covering all other evidence of human habitation.

At the end of the road stood Les Crane's Filling Station and Repair Shop, across from it, the bank, next to that, the cafe, the only establishments in town still in business. Beyond them, the grasses resumed, continuing as far as she could see.

In her journey Mavis did not see another human being. She didn't see or hear a car. She would have been surprised if she had. She was used to her solitude.

She walked behind the cafe, took a small bucket from its hook by the back door, hung it by the ribbon over her neck, and let herself through the mesh fencing into her overgrown patch of blueberries. They were the only item she could seize on when Nate asked her what it was about Michigan that she missed.

"Okay," he'd said, "you will have pies, and ice cream, and anything else you could possibly want."

He'd planted fifty bushes. Five would have been enough. A thousand wouldn't have recaptured for her the feeling of a place she was at home in.

She picked several quarts from the early bushes. The berries were round, ripe, succulent. She ate a few, took no pleasure from them. She was afraid she'd lost even her taste for fresh blueberries.

She climbed the back stairs to her apartment, set the bucket on the kitchen table. After supper she'd get out the cookbook, look over recipes, begin the daily game, "What shall I do with the excess?"

For supper she chose items that took a long time to prepare: blueberry muffins served with scrambled eggs and blueberries, with a blueberry milk shake to drink. She ate slowly, chewing every bite before swallowing. Lingering over blueberries wasn't easy.

She had already tried all the plausible recipes and many of implausible ones. For the evening she settled on blueberry pie, a batter for blueberry pancakes, more mixings for blueberry milk shake. To use up what she'd just picked she made a second pie, doubling the amount of blueberry called for in the recipe.

By the time she took the second pie out of the oven and put it on the windowsill to cool, the clock was striking nine. Nine hours to go.

She lit the lights. Outside it was growing darker. Before long the rest of the world would disappear. Her windows would border on blackness, and all the living universe would be compressed inside the walls of her apartment.

She could have flicked on the television but reception was so poor on the one channel she could get, her eyes hurt trying to figure out what the shapes were. For decent reception she needed a tower a hundred feet tall, or a satellite dish aimed at the sky, pulling in waves from invisible space. She couldn't afford either one.

She didn't like the two radio stations she could get. They seemed corny in a homespun South Dakota way she found annoying. When the radio started getting nothing but static she hadn't bother having it fixed.

She sat at the table, facing thinking time alone.

She thought first of Alice, where she might be, how long it'd been since Mavis had heard from her, if she might call. Mavis tried to imagine Alice's life—who she lived with, if she had friends, was she working, where, was there a man in her life. Was she in trouble? did she need help? would she turn to Mavis if she did? It was a little after eight in California, if that is where she was. Still light.

"Outside the window here"—she imagined a phone conversation to a daughter whose number she didn't know—"it's just gotten dark. Oh, and the first of the blueberries are ripe. Would you like me to send you some? Is there anything I can do for you? Are you coming for a visit sometime? What if I came out there? The change might do me good."

The conversation faded. Outside it was dark. The glass of the window reflected yellow light back into the room.

Alice's place was taken by Nate, dead—she could hardly believe it—eleven years. Every day at dark Mavis thought of him, still angry at him for bringing her to that desolate place and then leaving. She pleaded that he might return. She longed to sit with him, lie beside him, talk together, laugh, touch, be intimate—and, afterwards, lie entwined, contented, rubbing his skin, discussing something removed by thousands of miles from this wasteland. How unfair it was that he was gone, turning her life, so lush with him, barren.

Loving him, missing him, feeling sorry for herself that other women had their husbands but not her, she pictured him so vividly he stood in the door of the apartment, balding, wiry, stooped, aging but still handsome, witty, winning, what remained of his blonde hair and mustache streaked with white, a slight smile on his face, as if he'd come to share some pleasantry. She saw him in such detail that she half rose and said, as if she hadn't expected him back so soon, "Nate!"

She was talking to empty space.

She sat, waiting to hear the door shut behind him, his tread recede down the stairs, something besides the ticking of the clock.

She sat for so long she began to doubt whether she had called his name. Maybe she'd only imagined it. She began to wonder if she existed. What if she'd only imagined that too? Wasn't there a principle of physics that stated if there was no sound, there was no perceiver and therefore no existence, like absolute zero in temperature—total stillness indicating complete absence of life.

The idea of her not existing terrified her. What if she had disappeared that evening, ended up neither on earth nor wherever Nate was. She wanted to scream, to cry out, to prove she was living.

She opened her mouth, strained. No sound came out. What if one had? What would that prove? She could shout through a bullhorn and no one would hear. Only her, and she couldn't convince herself she hadn't imagined it.

She sat, not daring to move. Mentally she occupied less and less space, as if willing herself to disappear, until she felt her entire being could be held in the palm of her hand, like a glass ball.

She became aware of a sound. It seemed to expand, to fill the room. It wasn't the clock.

She held her breath. She heard nothing but the ticking of the clock. She resumed breathing. The noise resumed too. She did this several times. Each time the sound joined in, as if playing a game with her.

She decided there was one something alive in that room.

Maybe it was her.

She rose, walked toward the full-length mirror at the end of the apartment. The closer she approached, the greater her doubts. When she was near enough to see, she shut her eyes. She groped for the fabric drawer where she kept black scraps and remnants she had decorated the apartment with after Nate's death. She pulled an armful out, dumped them on the floor. She picked them up piece by piece, covered the mirror with them, the smaller mirror on a stand on her bureau, the windows, the glass-fronted case. She even laid pieces over the knives and spoons, felt with her hand to make sure she hadn't missed any.

When there was no reflective surface uncovered anywhere in the apartment, she reopened her eyes. She felt safe.

Mavis slumped down into a chair. From the edge of her senses she heard a clock strike. She counted. Eleven strokes. Seven more hours until morning.

Time to try to sleep, she decided. She washed up, brushed her teeth in the dark—she'd forgotten to cover the bathroom mirror. She looked around for something to read, found nothing she hadn't read five times before. She switched out the lights, walked into the bedroom.

She half expected to find Nate, sitting on his side of the bed, his feet on the floor, or lying in bed reading *A Geological History of South Dakota*. He'd been working his way through it a paragraph at a time when he died. "This is fascinating," he kept telling her, "so much I never knew." She had left it on his night stand, the marker still at the page where he'd stopped reading the night before he took the boat out fishing on the reservoir.

She had looked at it too. It was, if not fascinating, at least interesting. It gave her a sense of the formation of that strange land, millions of years earlier. All records of its past remained intact beneath the present, which was forming what would be the thin layer that was its own geological history and of which even she was a part.

She looked around the room, trying to imagine Nate moving

in it, naked, getting ready for bed, for lovemaking, talking, or sleep. She lay down, this image of him firmly in mind, as if by willing it she could bring him back. She toyed with her picture of him, smiled as he seemed to spring to life. She laid her hand across the covers to touch him, felt the coldness of his place.

Nate vanished. No matter how much she loved, missed, wanted him, she couldn't fantasize where there wasn't the remotest possibility of his return.

She lay, eyes shut, hoping to sleep. Her mind raced. She gave up trying.

She thought of Mort, the only remote possibility in her life—his sandy good looks, wry humor, thin frame, relaxed manner, his gentleness of being she found so attractive. She played out various scenarios, pretexts to lure him into her apartment, and once she had him there, locking him in, chaining him to the table, holding him prisoner, making him talk to her, of anything, of everything, while she listened, thought, argued, all the time watching how his mouth moved, his eyes darted as he thought until, in the midst of a passionate discussion, they succumbed to their feelings, and, respecting the memory of Mort's uncle, made love on the floor, on the table, couch. With expressions of "At last" and "You can't imagine how long I've waited for this," Mavis came. She felt waves of water flowing over her, like a shower soaking into parched earth, relaxing her being and her mind until the room, her imaginary lover, life and its troubles faded away and, vaguely aware of a clock in the distance striking twelve, she slept.

A waning moon rose over the southeastern hills, bathed the fields in a misty light. A soft breeze meandered along, swaying the back of a snake of tall grass, the warm-cool air it stirred promising another hot, dry day to come. From a cottonwood tree by a dry stream in the distance came the sound of an owl. On a hill to the south a coyote lifted his head and called. To his west, several hills over, another answered.

The one inhabitant of Grasslands slept. In her apartment the only noise that could be heard was the ticking of the clock and the rhythm of her breathing.

Mavis reentered the world of the conscious at three-fifteen A.M. She sat up in bed, staring out the uncovered window of her bedroom. Her hand pointed toward the empty lot across the road and the expanse of fields behind it. She saw them, in a dream so vivid she was sure were still there, filled with crowding, stamping, bellowing buffalo, a tangled mass of shapes and shadows in the moonlight, making so much noise the room shook.

The buffalo were being herded by a band of Indians riding bareback around the edges, throwing spears into their midst. From time to time one crumpled to the ground.

Shots rang out, filled the air. Two Indians fell from their horses. The rest galloped away. The shots continued. The knees of many bison buckled. They keeled over, lay on the ground, trying to rise, sinking lower, until their sides heaved one last time and their legs were still. The others gathered closer together and, stampeding, left, the ground shaking behind them.

A detachment of soldiers rode up. They shot at the remaining buffalo until none remained standing and rode on, still shooting.

Into this scene of carnage came a lone Indian on a white horse. He picked his way through piles of corpses of animals and Indians until he reached the place where the lot ended, at the edge of the road. Lifting up their heads, he and the horse stood in the moonlight, staring through walls and time directly at Mavis.

"No!" She shook her head, looked back out on the lot and field lying empty in the moonlight.

She reached out, took two white shank bones from the stand beside the bed. Clank, she hit them together. Clank clank. The noise echoed through the apartment, spread out into the darkness. Clank clank, clank clank. She got out of bed, stood swaying in the middle of the room, started moving her feet to the rhythm she was making. Clank clank, clank clank clank. She kept clanking them together, louder, wilder, filling the night with sound.

ABOUT THE AUTHOR

Jonathan Gillman is a graduate of Harvard College and the University of Minnesota, where he studied Theatre Arts and Playwriting. His plays have been produced in a variety of locations. His short stories have been published in the minnesota review, Short Story Review, Azorian Express, Albany Review, *and a number of other literary magazines. Since 1985 he has been the Head of the Drama Department, Greater Hartford Academy of the Performing Arts. He is also the Director of Looking In Teen Theatre. With his wife, Elizabeth, he lives on and works a farm in Connecticut.*